DINO HUNTERS

DISCOVERY IN THE DESERT

Written and co-created by
PETER LEAVELL

Illustrated and co-created by
KEN RANEY

RANEY DAY
PRESS

Grandma!
Thank you for
your love & support!

love,

[signature]

1/29/18

Dino Hunters: Discovery in the Desert

Published by Raney Day Press.

Cover and interior design by Ken Raney.

Printed in the United States of America.

Acknowledgments

Deb Raney for editing and her support.

Becky Lyles for edits and critiques.

Dr. Jerry Simmons, PHD Geology for his input and willingness to read the manuscript and offer constructive comments.

Robert Elmer, a successful Christian writer who has written dozens of novels for kids and adults, who read an early manuscript and gave us some great advice.

Landry Jordan, Cole Buckingham, Demian DeHoet, Jacob Stuhlsatz, and Ally Bishop for posing and modeling for Abby, Josh, David, Thomas, and Abby and Emma respectively. Are you ready to start on book 2?

CHAPTER ONE
April, 1925
Havasupai Canyon, Arizona

Josh pointed his dad's black camera and looked through the foggy window at evidence that would make him famous. *Josh Hunter, Thirteen-Year-Old Dinosaur Hunter* the headlines would declare. Most people loved reading about archeology in the newspapers as much as he did.

Josh lined up the shot, pointing the camera at the hot Arizona canyon floor, where a recent rainstorm had swept away the gravel.

Click.

He pushed his wide-brimmed hat off his forehead and wound the camera's dial, a metal circle atop the German-made device, and snapped another picture.

Click.

He took a step back, into the shade of the cave's entrance. The long but narrow canyon seemed to trap the heat, and the short willows that grew near the stream down the center offered the only other shade.

The dinosaur tracks led from the stream to the cave.

Now, what would archeologists want to see? What had Dad taught him? Josh had been so excited when his parents let him borrow the camera, he'd forgotten his lessons. And he rarely forgot anything. Ever. Mom and Dad were camped nearby. Should he get them?

Nah.

Right. A close-up of the tracks.

Click.

He wound the dial again.

He heard footsteps and didn't have to look up to recognize their rhythm. Abby, his eleven-year-old sister, was marching toward him.

"Attaboy, Josh!" Abby grabbed his arm.

Click.

"Abby! Stop it. You just made me take a picture of your face."

"Look, Josh. The dinosaur tracks have human tracks right beside them." Abby jumped up and down, flapping her arms like a duck, which would've been strange anywhere, but looked really odd in the middle of the desert. "You know what that means, right?"

Another image appeared in Josh's mind, an encyclopedia entry this time, the one that said humans and dinosaurs didn't coexist in the same time period. "Yeah, Abby. I know." He wound the film again.

She shook his shoulder. "Josh!"

Click.

"It means that dinosaurs and humans existed at the same time. We've got to find Mom and Dad!"

"I think I got a picture of my knee this time. Settle down." He turned from the camera. "There's work to do here."

"Right." Her bright eyes didn't dim. "What can I do?"

"I'm going to search the cave. You clear the gravel out of these tracks, where the water didn't touch."

Abby stripped off her jacket, revealing a short-sleeved shirt and muscles any eleven-year-old would be envious to own. Any eleven-year-old *boy*. Josh and Abby went on expeditions with Mom and Dad all the time, and while Abby seemed to get stronger with every climb and hike, Josh couldn't seem to keep up with his sister. His *little* sister.

She glanced out the entrance, seemed to spot what she was looking for, and rushed into the sunlight. With a flick of her wrist, she pulled an archeology brush from her bag, rested on one knee, and started to whisk away dirt.

Dust clouded around her face.

Josh smiled. *That should keep her busy for a bit.* He took off his hat and stepped into the cave. And another step. Careful, careful.

After about twenty short steps, just enough light at the entrance came through to see the cave wall.

He stopped and stared. Was that really...? He leaned closer.

At home, his parents shelved a new set of encyclopedias—Britannica. He'd read them, A-Z. Now, he used his near-perfect memory to call up the picture on the cave wall to match a page in the encyclopedia.

Ibex. These were ibex.

The creature was a deer-like animal from Africa. How did people on another continent, separated by oceans, know to paint them?

He lifted the camera to take a picture.

Click.

"You fiends!" Abby's voice shot through the cave.

Josh looked toward the entrance and didn't see Abby. He rushed toward the light and paused just inside the shadow.

Four men stood in a semi-circle, like a quarter moon, with Abby in the center. She faced them, hands on her hips, and she was giving them a piece of her mind.

The men wore strange clothes for the desert—black hats, black business suits and ties, and polished black shoes. One man was short and held a crowbar, another fat, gripping a pickax, and another tall and skinny, wielding a rifle. But the fourth, the one who seemed to be in charge, wore desert garb similar to Josh's. He wore an expensive Stetson with a leopard skin band, like a big game hunter might wear to a party. Braided string dangled around his neck, holding the hat in place. The man's hair was nearly white, blond really, and dropped under his hat and nearly fell into his eyes.

"Get to it," the blond man said. The three men in suits turned their attention to the tracks. Two lifted their tools and smashed the tracks, the air filling with the sound of metal striking rock.

"No!" Abby screamed, and with fists raised, she charged at the two men.

The third lifted his rifle, and she instantly slid to a halt.

"Put the rifle down. We're not shooting a little girl."

When the man lowered his gun, Abby leapt toward the men again.

The man with the blond hair grabbed her, and they became a whirl of arms and legs and screams. Finally, he held her on the ground, pinning her arms behind her back. "Keep working," he snarled.

Josh had to save Abby, but first, he needed evidence. These men would pay for destroying the fossil records. He waited until one of the men lifted a crowbar high, and as it smacked the rock, he snapped a picture. He covered the knob with his hand to quietly wind the film. Again, he waited to take the next picture until the sound covered the camera's snap.

And another picture.

And another.

Click.

The four men looked up.

He'd carelessly taken the shot between their strikes.

"Hey, he's got a camera!" The blond man pointed at Josh. "Get him!"

Abby struggled from the man's arms, shot out of his grip, and sprinted along the canyon bottom. The man with the rifle fired at her, the gunfire echoing against the walls and through Josh. His control vanished, and he raced after Abby.

The blond man shouted, "We don't shoot kids! Get after them, they've got pictures of us!"

Clutching the camera to his chest, Josh tore after Abby, and they sprinted down the canyon.

Was it one minute of running? Ten? A bazillion? Josh sensed they were racing toward their parents, but he wasn't sure how much longer he could run with the ache in his side, his wobbly legs, and his pouring sweat.

Thankfully, Abby paused at a fork in the canyon. "Which way, Josh? We've got to tell Dad!"

He glanced back. The men were still coming. "Split

up? Meet above the falls?"

Abby's face shadowed, then she smiled. "I remember them. See you there." She took off.

Josh headed the opposite direction. The desert sand squirted out from under his safari boots, making traction difficult. His breaths came in painful gasps. Desert scrub flashed by on either side. He came to a small stream, and followed the bright water downhill, deeper into one of the hundreds of canyons that eventually led to the Grand Canyon.

A huge lizard dashed out from under a bush and crossed his path.

He instinctively reached for the camera, but resisted the temptation. Why did he find the most interesting animals when running for his life? *The Children's Encyclopedia*, 1920 edition. Heloderma suspectum, of the class reptilia. Gila monsters bit. The venom from glands in its jaw wouldn't kill Josh, but he would get sick — and fall into the hands of the men chasing him. What if Abby was bit by a rattlesnake? What if the men found her, instead of him? He regretted leaving her to flee alone.

The lizard disappeared under a pile of rocks just as Josh planted his boot and leapt over a boulder to avoid the creature. Still running, he switched the camera to his other hand and wiped his palm against his canvas pants.

Cliffs of red rock towered above him on either side like giant crates, boxing him in. He skirted a bush, darting along the banks of the bright blue stream that cut through the desert.

The ache started in his side again and stretched into his lungs. How far had he run already? Twenty miles? Thirty? He must have been running for hours. Would he eventually have to run all the way down to the Grand Canyon?

He heard Abby call his name and looked up to see her hanging at the top of the cliff. From where he ran, the sheer canyon wall looked impossible to climb, but she scurried down the rock face like a spider, gripping invisible handholds.

He met her farther down the narrow canyon. "Josh, you've got to run faster," Abby chided. "They're going to catch us."

"I'm trying," he wheezed. "I've already run about two-hundred miles. Maybe even a bazillion." His breath came in gasps. He took off his hat and wiped his brow. His legs felt like noodles. He opened the lid of his round canteen and guzzled. Water trickled down his chin and onto his clothes.

"More like half a mile." Her red face and blonde ponytail were shaded under her pith helmet. "Did you lose them?"

He stumbled, kicking a rock into the water. "Not even Babe Ruth has to run this far, you know."

"Baseball players run every day. I don't think we lost them. Come on!" She sprinted away, leaving behind a cloud of dust.

He took a breath, coughed, and tore after her. When she slowed to let him catch up, he said, "We've got to get to Mom and Dad. Abby, if we're caught, they're going to steal the film. We've got to hide it before they kill us."

"It's 1925, Josh." She spoke over her shoulder. "People don't kill people like in the Dark Ages."

"So why are we running?" He pulled her arm to slow her down. He stopped and the stitch in his side lessened. He tugged the brim of his safari hat lower to block the sun and looked back the way they'd come. Four men, tiny dots, charged toward them.

A puff of dust jumped six feet in front of him. Thunder echoed through the canyon.

Abby jumped. "They're shooting at us. Go, Josh! Go!"

"We've got to get Mom and Dad," he repeated, and they took off.

They sprinted along the stream that bounced over rocks and around boulders. The water gurgled almost as loud as Josh's wheezing and pooled into a large, blue pond that reflected the cloudless Arizona sky. Strange, how he'd enjoyed creeks that wandered through the canyons before heading off to the Grand Canyon, and now he ran through them, trying to save himself and his sister.

He followed Abby around a cactus patch and through wildflowers.

She stopped, and he almost plowed into her. He dug his feet into the sand. Rocks shot into empty space, like the stream that burst over the edge of the cliff, crashing noisily into a deep pool below. The rotten egg smell of sulfur in the air was so strong he tasted it.

She gripped his arm as they looked over the edge. "That was close."

"Very close," he said as they took a step back.

"Josh, what do we do?" She let go of him and tugged at her pony tail. "We're trapped!"

He turned. The men were coming—now in the thick grove of trees along the stream. "I don't know."

"C'mon, Josh, you're the smart one." She made two fists. "I'll stay and fight them off. You get the camera out of the canyon." She swung her arm in an uppercut.

"Grown men, Abby! Four of them. And they have guns!"

"Remember Mitsuyo Maesa in Brazil? He taught me judo." But fear showed in her eyes now.

Josh looked up. On either side, cliffs soared higher than he could climb. He glanced behind, and the men burst from the trees, coming quickly. He turned and peered over the edge. Bad guys behind them, cliffs on either side, and a drop-off with waterfall in front of him.

He didn't want to say it, and definitely didn't want to do it. Another gunshot and dirt sprayed against his boots. "I've got an idea."

"What?"

"We go over the waterfall."

Abby leaned over the edge. "No way! That's a long drop!"

They had no other choice.

The falls. The name flashed in his memory. Havasu Falls. Ninety feet down.

He'd read when falling thirty feet or more, you needed the water to be twenty feet deep. The pool was high from spring runoff, probably twelve feet deep.

This was dangerous, too dangerous. But so were bullets.

"Go feet first, at a slight angle, and then curl underwater. When you come up, swim away from the waterfall before it pushes you under." He was a lousy runner, but swimming was something he could do.

"But what about the camera?"

She was right. The sulfur in the water would ruin the film. But he had an idea. "Here." He handed her the camera, then took a small round film canister from his pocket. "I can't say this is watertight." He shook the tin, rattling the unused film inside. "Can you climb down a ways and hide the tin?"

She looked back at the oncoming men and nodded.

"Quick, I need your bag."

"What?" She gripped the shoulder strap and turned away from him.

"I need to put the film in the canister. In the dark!"

She unslung the bag and handed to him.

He turned it upside down, and out fell a hand-sized trowel, a few baseball cards, a piece of licorice, four rocks, a sketch pad, and a dozen pencil stubs. And, thankfully, a rag.

He set the camera inside the bag, and worked the back of the camera with both hands. "Take that rag and cover where my hands are."

She snatched the cloth and did her best to block the light.

"If light touches the film—no pictures."

With sweaty fingers, he opened the camera, a brand-new Leica I, just out. He pulled out the film, rewound it, then shoved it into the round tin. He screwed the lid closed. "Done."

Abby snatched the items scattered around, filled her satchel, grabbed the canister, and started down the sheer canyon wall. She wouldn't be able to go far. The stone undercut the waterfall and made climbing the whole way impossible. Her head disappeared over the edge.

The men were close. He would have to jump at an angle to hit the middle of the pool. *God,* he prayed, *strike those men dead, so I don't have to jump.*

"Put your hands up or I'll shoot!" A man called out.

He would have to jump. *God, help me not to break all my bones. And help Abby. Keep her safe.*

Don't look, he whispered, *just go. Now.* He charged for the edge, ignoring his pounding heart and his mind that shouted *stop!*

He launched into the sky, boots like lead, leading the way straight down like an anchor. His yell reverberated between the canyon walls. "Nooooooo!" He flapped his arms like a bird.

The camera bounced hard against his chest.

Just before he hit the water, he heard his sister yell from above. "Yeeeeehaw!"

Abby. Could she really be enjoying this?

Frigid water enveloped him. His boots slammed into the bottom of the pool and he kicked upward.

He burst through the surface, gasping for air. A sulfur taste filled his mouth. He sputtered and spit out water.

Abby popped up beside him, giggling. "That was fun!"

"Are you serious?" He reached his floating hat, then made his first stroke toward the edge. "I never want to do that again." At least, not with people chasing them.

The waterfall seemed to pull them back as they swam to the shore, but soon they stamped out of the pool. Abby grabbed her helmet and continued down the smooth, gravel path along the canyon. He looked far above them at the rim, over the waterfall. One man held a rifle on his hip. The rest just stood there, watching.

He and Abby jogged around a bend in the ravine, already drying in the warm April sun. After a few minutes, his shaking body relaxed.

The canyon widened, and the path split into two. They turned away from the stream.

"Look," Abby shouted, "There's Mom and Dad." She sprinted across a wide-open valley dotted with scraggly scrub.

Dad sat at his field desk next to their tent, while

Mom cooked in the fire pit. The rest of the expedition — ten tents in all — was empty. Everyone else must be working in the field.

Josh shouted, "Mom! Dad!"

Mom looked up from the fire and waved, then turned and said something to their dad, whose back was to them. He looked up from his desk.

Mom and Dad walked toward them, skirting brush, rocks and cactus. They met in the shade of a mesquite tree. Their mother gave them each a quick hug. "What happened? You seem all aflutter."

Josh tried to talk, but the terror of the morning finally caught up with him, and he couldn't form the words.

Abby spoke in jagged clumps through heaving breaths. "We were in a canyon. One we haven't worked in before. Farther up." She took a deep breath. "We found a shallow cave."

Josh managed, "By the Havasu stream bed."

"Water had washed away most of the gravel." Abby took off her helmet and wiped her damp forehead with her sleeve. "You know how you told us footprints made in mud can harden into rock?"

"Dinosaur tracks," Josh exclaimed. "Right next to human tracks." He looked from his mom to his dad. "In the same strata!"

Abby clapped her hands. "Side by side! Can you believe it?"

Dad's right brow rose, a sign he was intrigued. "Which dinosaur was it? Did you recognize it?"

"Coelophysis," Josh said. "I'm pretty sure it was a

Coelophysis. I also saw a wolf's track in the rock."

"And then..." Abby took a step forward. "Josh found paintings on the cave wall and —"

"Ibex!" Josh had to be the one to tell them. "Ibex, being chased by the Coelophysis. But then —"

"Four men with crowbars demolished the human tracks we just discovered." Abby settled her helmet on her head and smacked it with her palm. "We didn't even have time to do a full study on the tracks."

"Dad, Mom..." Josh looked at them. "They chiseled the tracks out of the stone. Just smashed them to smithereens."

"But Josh took pictures." Abby indicated the soggy camera. "Pictures of the paintings. And the men. Then they saw us, and came after us." She took a quick breath. "We got away, but they followed. And they're coming now. Dad, they shot at us!" She spun, looking over her shoulder.

Josh looked, but no one was there. "We've got to run. Or stop them." Suddenly, he wished all fifty members of their expedition were here. Those bad guys wouldn't be so brave when they had to face Dad and their leader, Dr. Hubbard.

Mom grabbed Dad's arm, her face red and angry. "What should we do? They fired bullets at them, Peter! Real bullets! What kind of men shoot at children?"

"The kind of men that are going to regret coming here at all." Dad snatched a trowel from his desk and slammed it into the ground. He looked at the tent and thought for a moment. "No one shoots at anyone and gets away with it."

"What are we going to do?" Mom whispered. Josh noticed her hands shook as much as his did.

"Martha, take the children to the edge of camp. Dr. Hubbard and Mr. Doheney are back for a short visit before they start their speaking tour again, so I'll tell them what's going on, then I'm hiking you and the kids out of here and to the car."

The hike out was miles. Six miles.

"Fill canteens," Dad said as he entered the tent. Josh could still hear his instructions through the white canvas. "Take jerky and peanuts and raisins." He opened the flap and stepped out with a rifle in his hands. He settled the barrel on his shoulder so it pointed into the sky. "Leave the fire and the beans. There's no time. I'll be back in a few minutes."

Twenty minutes later, Dad returned. Mom led, then Abby, followed by Josh. Dad brought up the rear, and they passed through camp, skirted a mountain of supply crates, then took the narrow trail toward the car, moving South, up, and out of the vast canyon network.

They passed a few workers returning to camp, all confirming they'd heard from another person to get to camp and arm themselves.

After ten minutes of hiking, they saw no one else.

"You said you stashed the film behind the waterfall?" Dad asked as they marched.

"In case they caught us, yeah."

Josh turned, and checked his father's face to see if he was mad. But he seemed more preoccupied, keeping an eye on the cliffs around them.

Dad looked grim. "In this heat, I'm not sure how

long the film will last. But behind the waterfall, it should stay cool. That was good thinking, Josh."

He hadn't said a word about the ruined camera. "Thanks, Dad."

Six miles later, the canyon smoothed out, and soon Josh spotted the car where they'd stopped when the canyon became too rocky for automobiles.

Josh swung the door open and climbed into the driver's seat, exhausted after the long hike.

"In back, Josh!"

Josh crawled over the seat into the back as Dad jumped into the front. In seconds, they raced down the road. Josh turned to see a huge dust trail behind them. They barreled down the single lane that cut like an arrow across the desert.

The only sound was the wind that blew through the open windows.

"Maybe they weren't trying to kill us," Josh ventured, now that he felt safe. "Maybe they were just after the film and wanted to scare us. They missed us after all."

Josh looked at Abby to see her reaction. She shrugged and offered a smirk. Then she laughed out loud. "Other than the guns, that was fun!"

Josh had to admit, the adventure *had* been fun. It would be hard to top men shooting at them. But something in his gut told him that life was about to get even more interesting.

CHAPTER TWO
April, 1925 - Five Days Later
Colbey, Tennessee

*D*octor David Hunter strode down the hallway of the Biology Building toward his office and a waiting phone call.

He barely glanced at a display of a stuffed grizzly bear when a blond man in a gray suit stepped in front of him, blocking his way.

"Dr. Hunter," the man said with a scowl.

"Thomas," he replied. "Please, I told you. Just call me David. Like everyone else."

"And you may call me Professor Thomas." He crossed his arms. "It's important to acknowledge a well-earned title, so people will honor education."

David chuckled. "All, right, I'll humor you professor."

"I just heard your lecture on mammals. And I must say, I'm very upset."

David glanced down the hallway toward the entrance where students filled the space, moving quickly to the next class. Through an opening in the mass of bodies, he saw his secretary, Emma, hold up an imaginary telephone receiver to her ear, indicating that his call was still waiting. Her expression said he should hurry.

He motioned past the man. "Professor Thomas, I have a call—from my niece in Arizona—and I don't know how long the operator will hold."

"Your niece can wait." Professor Thomas shoved him back a step.

David regained his balance and rose to his full six-foot height. "Now see here—"

"You think you're some kind of king? First, you write a book about evolution. Then you tell your students you have doubts about Darwin's theories?"

"I'm second guessing the timeline is all. Nothing to be

upset over." David shrugged. He wanted to say he was the author of the bestselling book *Evidences and Substantiation of Darwin's Theory*, and that he had every right to guess. But that would sound arrogant. "All I said was that everything evolves, so I'm wondering why we have ferns in fossil records that are identical to ferns we have today. A plant didn't evolve."

Thomas shook his head. Long strands of hair fell in his face, and he brushed them back with one hand. "We can't be showing doubt. Not when teaching evolution is under attack."

"The weather suggests they should have evolved. Surely you're not suggesting we scientists should deny concrete evidence. Besides, we must question all theories. Test everything. Even our own theories. Now, my apologies, but I must go."

Professor Thomas took a step back. "Our responsibility is to teach our students *what* to think. Otherwise, they might formulate all the wrong ideas about science."

Unbelievable. Teaching students what to think went against everything David believed. He shook his head and whisked past Professor Thomas.

Display cases filled with the Biology Department's finest treasures lined the hallway. Dinosaur bones, a monkey skull, and several ocean specimens floated in jars of formaldehyde. A massive collection of butterflies had been pinned to boards. Over a dozen mounted animals, including monkeys, lions, bears, and even a rhinoceros stood guard over the students. Birds, mountain lions, and other animals featured in dioramas of their natural habitats made this building the most visited at Colbey College.

David entered the secretary's office. All he could see was the bobbing feather atop Emma's hat. He heard a clicking typewriter and leaned over the tall counter that surrounded her desk.

Emma glanced up. "David."

Her broad smile and sparkling blue eyes never failed to move him. That was why he'd asked her to marry him last month. And she had agreed right away.

He offered a grin that usually made her smile. "A student said you have a phone call for me."

"Yes!" Emma spun and grabbed the phone, lifting it to him. "Long distance."

He brought the receiver to his ear, held the mouthpiece in front of his lips, and expecting to talk to the operator, used his deep, professional voice. "This is Dr. Hunter."

He heard a crackle, then a soft, "Uncle David?"

"Abby?" He could barely make out her voice. She was his favorite niece—probably because she was his only niece. And Josh was his only nephew. The two belonged to his only brother, Peter. "Aren't you in Arizona?"

"Uncle David?" This time her voice was clearer.

"Yes, Abby, I'm here."

She began to sob.

"Sweetie, what's wrong?" He gripped the stick phone.

"Uncle David…" She sobbed again and his heart broke for her. "Mom and Dad are dead."

Her words slammed like a lightning bolt into his head and heart. "Abby? What did you say?" Maybe he'd heard wrong.

"Mom and Dad died."

He slumped against the counter. "Abby." All he could manage was a whisper. "What happened?"

"It was a car accident. Josh and I are okay, but…" Her words faded into sobs.

A man's voice came on the line and asked if this was Mr. Hunter.

"Where is Josh? What's going on?"

"That boy won't stop arguing with me about his parents in an accident. Thinks they were murdered. Had to lock him up. Now, are you Mr. Hunter?"

"Yes, I'm David Hunter." His own voice sounded hollow and far away. "You *locked up* Josh?"

"I'm sheriff of Mohave County, Arizona. These kids are pretty shook up, as you can imagine. They need someone. Family. Someone's got to look after them or they go to an orphanage. You that someone?"

He was the kids' only living relative, other than his mother, who was in no condition to care for children.

He heard himself say, "Yes—"

"Fine then," the sheriff said. "We're putting them on a train headed your way right now."

"No. I'll come get them." David forced his mind to work. He could fly the drugstore owner's plane. "I can be there tomorrow."

"Sorry, they're already out the door."

"Wait—"

"We ain't paying for their train ticket. Means you're going to have to repay us."

"Money is not a problem," David stammered.

"Well…" The sheriff drew out the word. "Might not be for you eastern folk, but out here—"

"Send me the bill, Colbey College Biology Department." His brother had died, and this man wanted to discuss money? "Just…just get them here."

"And there's a fee for housing them for the past several days—"

"Days! You've had the kids for a few days? My brother's been dead for a few days, and you're just now telling me?"

He heard Emma gasp.

"Now see here, watch your tone— I'll send you a bill."

David heard a click. He slowly hung up the phone.

Emma touched his arm. "What is it, David?"

"Help me get the train station on the line. In Mohave County, Arizona."

She took the phone and called the local operator. While she waited to be connected, she asked. "What's happened?"

"My brother and his wife are dead. Car accident, apparently. Josh and Abby are on a train, headed to Tennessee to live with me." He stared at her. "What are we going to do?"

Emma tilted her head to the receiver, listening. "All right. Thanks, Donna."

"No one answers at the station." Emma's eyes filled with tears, then a firm look of determination and strength hardened her features. She stood, and grabbed his hand. "We're going to do what's best for them."

"I'm a father now." And he thought of his dead brother

and closed his eyes as pain filled his heart.

CHAPTER THREE

May, 1925 - One Month Later
Colbey, Tennessee

Sprawled across his uncle's couch, Josh stuck his hands behind his head and frowned at his sister sitting on the floor, almost nose to nose with him. "I don't want to go visit the college. Or Uncle David. I'm fine right where I'm at."

"You never want to go anywhere anymore, Josh!"

Her loud voice made his ears ring.

But Josh didn't move. He was sticking to his guns, no matter what she said. "No, I don't. And I'm okay with that."

"It's been a month since Mom and Dad died, Josh. Come

on… The walk will do you good."

"No, Abby, it won't. A walk won't bring Mom and Dad back." He swiped at the tears that trickled down his cheek. No matter how hard he tried, he couldn't stop them.

She leaned her chin on the cushion. "I guess it may be harder for you, since you're older than I am and knew Mom and Dad better?"

He stared at the ceiling, clamping his jaw and his fists in a useless effort to keep his emotions in check.

"You still can't see any encyclopedia pages in your mind? How about 'T' for Tennessee? After all, it's our new state."

He shook his head, wishing he'd never told her how his memory worked.

"I'm worried about you, Josh. Do you want me to make you a sandwich?"

He closed his eyes and rolled away from her. She sighed, and he heard her walk across Uncle David's living room and out the front door. Maybe he was the only one in the world who still cared for his mom and dad.

Abby wrapped her arms around herself. Although the spring day was sunny and clear, it was also chilly. A car passed by, and the driver turned to look at her. She stared back. *Yes, this is a boy's shirt.* But it made so much more sense than those silly frills most girls wore. Climbing trees in a glossy shirt with tassels cramped her style, since it resulted in many torn clothes. Her father had always been proud of her adventurous spirit.

She wandered down the street, past houses that looked

similar to Uncle David's small home, past flower gardens and white picket fences. Large trees lined the street, their roots tilting sidewalk slabs in crazy slopes. She leapt over a gaping hole where the sidewalk was missing a square.

In the distance stood Uncle David's college. The buildings lay in the bright morning light like a small city. If she remembered right, her uncle's building was on the closest corner. Maybe she'd peek in the window of his classroom. Surely, no one would care.

They'd visited the college with Mom and Dad several times.

She crossed the street, found Uncle David's building, and studied the hedge that ran beneath his classroom windows. A tree rose from the bushes. The windows were open. If she climbed the tree, she'd be able to listen to Uncle David lecture.

She scrambled up the tree's evenly spaced branches. The scent of fresh flowers wafted up from the hidden petals behind the bushes. She looked down, and it seemed as if the gardener had lost complete control of the garden. Who ever heard of flowers behind bushes? She held a finger under her nose to stop the sneeze that threatened to explode. Finally, the tickle calmed, and she climbed a little higher and peeked inside.

Chalkboards lined the front of Uncle David's classroom. A single, wide desk sat beneath them, with an easel off to one side. The door to the classroom was on the opposite wall.

Dozens of students sat in long rows of chairs set on platforms that rose higher and higher until they reached the back of the room.

"We've learned so much through science," Uncle David

was saying.

Abby leaned closer. She loved science…well, obviously since it had been her parents' career as archeologists.

Her uncle stepped away from his desk and picked up a piece of chalk. On the chalkboard, he wrote one word: *evolution*. "As you know, Charles Darwin wrote *On the Origin of Species by Means of Natural Selection* in 1859." He held out a hand. "There's more to the title. *Or the Preservation of Favoured Races in the Struggle for Life*." Some in the class laughed. "Even though the book has some errors, Darwin's book is compelling, a good start to scientific thinking about how we humans came to exist on Planet Earth.

Abby's heart sank. Uncle David was a fervent believer in evolution. The books and fossils scattered about his house were a constant reminder of his passion.

A student raised his hand.

Uncle David ran his fingers through his dark hair. "Yes?"

"The Bible clearly says we were *created* by God. We didn't evolve from apes. You can't convince me my family tree has monkeys in it."

Uncle David turned to the chalkboard and wrote another word: *fact*. "In science, especially in biology, we study one word. *Fact*. What we can see with our eyes. We used to guess what happened to a cell, but now, with powerful microscopes…" He pointed to the three microscopes on a table under the windows. "We can actually see what takes place."

Uncle David looked so calm and smooth up front, Abby couldn't help but be impressed. "The creation theory falls into the realm of myth," he said. "It's based solely on sacred writings found in the Bible, which teaches faith and morality and encourages people to do good. But the Bible is not a science book."

Abby couldn't breathe. Her father and Uncle David had gotten into many arguments about the differences between creation and evolution. She'd hoped her uncle would see the truth, but that apparently hadn't happened. Yet.

Dr. Hunter leaned against his desk. "Science searches for evidence. Measure and observe. The creation myth cannot be verified because none of us were there to observe it. We need natural evidence."

"Was anyone there to observe monkeys turning into men?" The student who'd defended his family tree shot back without waiting to be called on.

Hands shot up all over the room.

Uncle David ignored them and walked to the easel, pulling out posters until he found the one he needed. "This is a drawing of an Archaeopteryx, which died out long ago, the earliest bird fossil discovered. Today, we still have birds, but they are different than this extinct one. What makes these changes in their biological makeup? God or natural selection?"

Abby was having a hard time understanding what he meant. Josh would know. She'd ask him. She glanced at the students. Two dozen hands were up now.

She listened to their questions. Uncle David patiently answered them all. Then the bell rang and the students filed out the door.

When no one came into the room for the next class, she started down the tree.

"David."

The authoritative voice came from inside the room. She scrambled back up the branches and peered inside again. The

Dean of the Science Department was standing at the door. She'd met him once, and he was nice enough. Dr. Michaels? Was that his name?

Uncle David, who was bent over his leather briefcase, jumped to his feet, knocking over the globe on his desk. But he snatched the globe before it crashed to the floor. "Dr. Michaels."

Yep, that was the man's name.

"Oh, to be that young and quick again."

Uncle David tapped the globe and smiled.

Should she be listening to a private conversation? Snooping on a class was one thing, but—

"You keep rising in the biology world, Professor Hunter, and you'll be able to afford a hundred globes." Dr. Michaels stepped into the classroom and adjusted his spectacles. "How are things going?"

She was about to drop from the last branch to the ground, when she heard, "I mean, how are the children?"

Abby paused, then rose high enough to see in.

Her uncle sighed and rubbed his forehead. "The children seem healthy enough. Obviously deeply hurt. Abby smiles now and then, but Josh is stone-faced."

"Are you going to put them in school?"

Abby lifted her chin to hear better.

"My brother and his wife taught the kids themselves. They're both smart. I'm convinced Josh could take classes here at the university and excel, even though he's only thirteen. But healing takes time." He shuffled papers around on his desk. "I understand. I struggle with my brother's death. I miss him and his wife." After pausing, he said, "I'll talk to Josh and Abby about school this weekend."

Dr. Michaels adjusted the glasses on his narrow nose and offered a reassuring smile. "Perhaps you could invite the children to your special club." He lifted a hand, cutting off her uncle's objection. "I know they're young. But they need some social activities to keep their minds busy."

"Perhaps, perhaps." Uncle David set his briefcase on his desk. "I can't help but think the kids are hiding something. I often catch them cutting off their conversations when I enter the room."

Abby's heart skipped a beat. *Does he know about the film?* They'd almost told several times. Josh had thought it best not to tell adults, since chances were, they wouldn't believe them. That police officer in Arizona hadn't, and while most lawmen were nice, that one hadn't been. Besides, Mom and Dad knew about the film, and they'd been *killed*. Josh said by keeping the secret, they were keeping people safe.

"No matter. Probably just part of keeping their emotions inside. They'll tell you in good time. How long do you think you'll have them, David? You're going to be married, after all. And my daughter can't be kept waiting." He laughed.

So this was Miss Emma's father? They'd met Uncle David's fiancée a few times, but only briefly. She seemed fun. And nice. She'd make a good mom. But her mind reeled with all the new information. *Uncle David didn't plan to keep them?* Was he going to send her and Josh away when he married Miss Emma?

Uncle David frowned. "Emma is deciding a date, not me."

"Since Emma lost her mother a few years ago, she's been somewhat… distracted. She wants to help people, and I think she should be focused on her education."

Doctor Michaels folded his arms. "I wanted to talk to you

about one more thing, David."

"Sure." Her uncle copied the dean's stance.

"You have a bright future, and I'm pleased to know I'll be calling you my son-in-law one of these days."

"And I'll be pleased to call you my father-in-law."

"That will happen soon enough. But someday, you'll have my position as Dean of Science, and you'll have important decisions to make." He laughed. "Don't look so surprised. You've got the ability to go far, very far. But I need to discuss a delicate matter."

"Go ahead."

"Our state legislature has passed a law that teaching evolution in high schools is illegal."

"I've heard," Uncle David said. "The Scopes Monkey Trial."

"Exactly. Dr. Michaels waved his arms. "John Scopes has been arrested for teaching evolution. He's going to trial over in Dayton. What happens with the Scopes trial will have a profound effect on science education in this state. Perhaps the nation." He pointed a finger at Uncle David. "I want you to watch the trial closely. See if you can help the defense. The publicity and contacts you make will be good for you and for Colbey College."

Uncle David turned toward the windows. He looked straight at Abby. She gripped the branch. Would he punish her for spying on him? At first he looked shocked, but then he grinned and called, "Abby, Come inside!"

She released her grip on the branch and jumped, landing in soft dirt. After she brushed dust from her knees, she scurried around the building and entered the chilly hall. She couldn't help but glance at the stuffed animals. Taxidermy, Josh called it. She paused at the giant rhinoceros. *How did they stuff that? It's huge.*

Walking to Uncle David's classroom, which was down the hall and to the right, she caught a whiff of alcohol disinfectant, probably from biological experiments. She shivered.

She heard heels clicking against the tile floor and turned to see Miss Emma. Her cloche hat covered most of her light, bouncing hair. And her brown dress ended just below her knees, far higher than Mom and Dad let Abby wear her skirts—not that they'd often been able to convince her to wear one of the two dresses she'd owned. Those dresses were still back in Oklahoma, but she hadn't needed to wear one yet. She was thankful Uncle David didn't seem to care how she dressed.

"Abby! Now this is a pleasant surprise." Miss Emma engulfed her in a hug that felt almost as good as her mother's hugs. Abby closed her eyes.

"Are you here to see David?" Miss Emma drew away and moved her pocketbook from her hand to under her arm.

Abby winced. "He caught me peeking in his classroom window. I hope I'm not in trouble."

"Fiddle faddle. Come, let's go see him." Emma offered an elbow, and Abby wrapped her hand around her soon-to-be aunt's outstretched arm.

As they entered the room, Dr. Michaels smiled and leaned over to kiss Miss Emma's cheek.

"Hello, Papa." Her smile turned into a shy grin when she looked to Uncle David. Rosy color touched her cheeks. "Hi, professor."

Uncle David grinned from ear to ear before kissing Miss Emma on the opposite cheek.

Abby rolled her eyes. Josh would be gagging about now.

As it was, she felt a little sick.

Miss Emma giggled. "David, have you forgotten?" She looked down at Abby. "Not in front of the children."

Abby groaned.

Uncle David looked at her. "I'm glad you came by, Abby. Feel free to visit anytime." He lifted his suit jacket from the back of his chair and pulled it on. "Josh didn't come with you, did he?"

"No."

"Miss Emma and I are eating lunch together. Would you like to join us? Maybe call Josh?" He glanced at Miss Emma. "If that's all right with you, of course."

She smiled and nodded. "I'll telephone him." Miss Emma grinned and hurried to her office.

Uncle David leaned down. "Since we installed a telephone in the department a few months ago, she's had a good time calling people and taking calls."

Abby hoped Josh would pick up and agree to join them.

Uncle David turned to Dr. Michaels. "And you?"

"No, I've papers to grade. You all have a good time." He returned Abby's gaze with a frown that made her think he didn't like her very much.

How could this man be Miss Emma's father? She was so kind, so relaxed. They looked somewhat alike, with their strong chins and upturned noses—although his dark hair was graying. The difference was how stiff he held his back. Miss Emma seemed to swivel like a fishing lure, and she hooked people into liking her. Abby knew all that from just the few times she'd seen her.

Unlike Miss Emma, Dr. Michaels didn't seem genuine. Was he the kind of person who was sometimes nice, sometimes mean?

The dean cleared his throat as he kept looking at her. "Your trip to Oklahoma to visit your parent's house..." He offered a gentle smile. "Did the visit bring back good memories?"

Abby wrapped her arms around her midsection and looked away. The tears she'd forgotten for the moment nearly started again. She didn't dare respond, for fear she might start crying again, and once she allowed herself to cry, she couldn't stop the tears.

"We started the long drive to Oklahoma," Uncle David said, "but we had to turn around. None of us are ready to visit Peter and Mary's home quite yet. But that's okay. The house will still be there, waiting for us, when we're ready to go inside."

Abby gave her uncle a grateful smile.

While the grownups talked, she kept an eye on the skeleton that hung from the ceiling on the other side of the microscopes. She waited for a hand to move.

It didn't.

"Hello, Professor Thomas." Miss Emma's voice came from the hallway.

A man with a smooth deep voice said, "Emma, you're looking beautiful today. Would you like to have lunch with me?"

Out of the corner of her eye, Abby saw Uncle David stiffen.

"Thank you, Professor Thomas, but I'll be lunching with David." Emma's voice took on an edge Abby hadn't heard before. "Remember, he and I are engaged to be married."

Professor Thomas chuckled. "For now, maybe. But I intend to marry you."

Uncle David took a step toward the door. Abby grinned.

Good for Uncle David. He'd teach that rude man some manners.

But before her uncle could exit the room, Emma's father grabbed his arm. "Let's keep peace in the Biology Department, shall we?" he whispered. "I'm sure he's just trying to get your goat. Professor Thomas has been here nearly a whole semester, and you two went to school together. Let it go."

Uncle David's face turned red and his jaw twitched, but he nodded and stepped back. Miss Emma's heels clicked toward them, and as she stepped into the room, he leaned down and whispered to Abby, "His name is Thomas Thomas."

Abby giggled, but couldn't hold back her disappointment that Uncle David hadn't taught that man some manners. She wondered what Professor Thomas looked like.

"What are you two laughing about?" Miss Emma asked, hands on her hips.

"Can't I share a secret with my favorite niece?" He patted Abby's head. "Did Josh answer?"

Abby held her breath. *Oh, please, please say he answered.*

"The operator tried three times. He finally picked up and said he would meet us at Mack's Diner in a few minutes."

Abby exhaled. Maybe, just maybe, her brother would be okay.

CHAPTER FOUR
May 1925 - Later That Afternoon
Colbey, Tennessee

Josh shuffled through Colbey College's Biology Building, head down. He glanced at the butterfly collection, but ignored the rest. Why should he keep looking? Normally, just a glance brought up all sorts of information in his head. Now, nothing.

Abby skipped by his side.

They'd gone to lunch, and then Uncle David had insisted they join him later for a club meeting at the college.

He didn't feel like going. But Abby had begged him to

join her. At least she wasn't talking. But every few steps she bumped into him.

Why did colleges all smell the same? Dad, who was an archeologist, had been asked to speak at several colleges across the country. Sometimes, he and Mom and Abby had gone with him. Every time, the buildings smelled of old wood, book dust, and girls' perfume. Why did girls wear perfume, anyway?

Each step through a building reminded him of his parents, and felt like a trowel dug at his heart. *God, why did You take my parents?*

As they followed students walking toward Uncle David's classroom, Josh knew the answer to his question. He had no idea why. That might not even be for him to know. And Josh knew he had to be okay with not knowing. Sometimes, though, it felt like too much. He quickly asked God to forgive his questioning doubts.

"I'm nervous about the Darwin meeting, Josh," Abby said. "From what I heard earlier today, Uncle David still believes evolution."

Josh shrugged, removed his cap, and put one hand in his pocket. He'd sit through the meeting, do what his uncle wanted, then go home to his room.

They were passing the roaring grizzly bear when Abby grabbed his shoulder and pointed.

No. It couldn't be.

He whisked off his cap, grabbed her arm, pulled her behind the bear. He leaned out to peer down the hall.

"Abby! It's him."

She dropped to her knees and peeked around the bear's legs. "I know!"

"He's the man from the desert. The one not dressed like a mobster."

"Fiddlesticks, Josh!" But then she looked again, and her eyes went wide. "It *is* him," she whispered.

The man's blond hair had been covered in a pith helmet last time they'd seen him. And he'd worn khakis, rather than the light gray suit he wore now. But it was the same man. Josh was positive. And what was worse, he stood right outside Uncle David's classroom door, talking to Miss Emma!

His sister stood and turned to him. Their faces were only inches apart. Her breath smelled like the peppermint they'd had after eating at Mac's. "Josh, we've got to tell Uncle David."

Josh looked back at the classroom door. Uncle David shook the evil man's hand, but he wasn't smiling the way he usually did when he talked with people.

He and Abby strained to hear their voices down the hall.

"Professor Thomas," Uncle David said as the evil man walked past him and into the classroom. Their uncle offered Miss Emma a kiss, then followed him inside.

"Josh!" Abby squealed, then lowered her voice to a whisper. "That's the new professor, Professor Thomas! And you know what? He wants to marry Miss Emma, too!"

Josh rubbed his chin. What to do? Finally, he said, "We've got to keep an eye on him. I'm not entirely sure he'll recognize us. I mean, you look a little different in your field gear. When we get a chance, we'll tell Uncle David. But not right now. Professor Thomas can't do anything to us with so many people around." He squeezed her arm. "Let's go."

They left their hiding place as Miss Emma walked by. "Hey you two. They're just about to start. I'm heading home to finish some work. See you tomorrow?"

Abby gave her a hug, and Miss Emma tousled Josh's hair before leaving.

They hurried down the hall and into Uncle David's classroom. The setting sun threw orange and red light against the faded wooden chairs. A skeleton hung from a wire, and even though the bones weren't real, it gave Josh a jolt. He wouldn't want to meet up with that skeleton at night.

The first three rows were filled with students, and Josh was glad they were busy joking with each other so didn't seem to notice him. Or Abby.

Josh spotted Professor Thomas in the second row, one leg crossed over the other, his arms stretched over the seats on either side of him.

Uncle David stood behind his desk.

"Uncle David." Abby smiled.

"How are you?" Uncle David hugged Abby and then roughed up Josh's hair.

Josh couldn't hold back a smile. But he whispered, "I need to talk to you. Right now."

Uncle David's brows furrowed. "It can't wait?"

From the corner of his eye, Josh saw Professor Thomas stand and move to the center aisle.

Josh exchanged glances with Abby. They couldn't talk with him around.

"Yes, Josh?"

"Um…"

Professor Thomas joined them at the front, Abby stepped away from the window, the late afternoon sunlight splashing against her back. She spoke in a loud voice. "I'm a bit of a sap. I couldn't get the electric toaster to work." She glanced nervously at Josh, then shook her head. "I'll never get the hang of not burning bread."

"You're no sap." Uncle David laughed. "Your slang sounds like one of my students."

Professor Thomas turned to Uncle David. "Dr. Hunter, are these young people your niece and nephew? They seem like a nice pair."

"Thank you." Uncle David's voice was surprisingly cold. He pointed to the front row and softened his tone. "Josh, Abby, you can sit there, if you like." He turned his back to them and faced the chalkboard and started writing.

1. Scopes Trial

Professor Thomas squinted, curled his lips, and whispered, "I hope you enjoy the class." He stretched the *s* into a hiss. "I'd hate for anyone to get hurt by telling lies about the desert. I trust you haven't told anyone."

Josh's mouth went dry. The professor recognized them!

"No." Abby stared up at him. "Did you kill my parents?"

Josh elbowed her. "Abby…"

"My dear," the man said quietly. "I was on a train for spring break, back to Colbey, when your parents died…"

Professor Thomas paused as he looked toward the students who ignored them, and Uncle David, who was writing on the board again.

2. Fruit Fly Experiments

He resumed. "Now, about those pictures. I trust you haven't developed them?"

Josh grabbed Abby's wrist and tugged her toward the front seats. He sat and glared up at the man.

Professor Thomas returned to his seat and resumed his nonchalant posture, a smirk twisting the corners of his mouth. All Josh could think was that he needed to figure out what to do next. His sister cupped her hand beside his ear and whispered, "Do you think he'll try to hurt us?"

Josh rubbed his forehead. *No, surely not.* But then, he remembered the evil look on the man's face and his veiled threat. "I doubt it," he murmured. "What would be the purpose?" *The pictures.*

Uncle David turned from the blackboard, and the voices in the room quieted. He reached into his vest pocket and pulled out his watch, which was attached to a belt loop by a long gold chain. He flipped the watch lid open. "Yes, time to start." He returned the watch to his pocket and smiled at the group.

"Welcome to the Darwin Club. Today, we're going to discuss the upcoming trial against Mr. Scopes, who taught evolution to his high school class and was arrested last month."

Someone shouted, "A travesty!"

A murmur of laughter filled the room.

Josh tried to focus on the discussion. He'd have to talk with his uncle later. They were safe for now.

"Perhaps." Uncle David lifted a hand. "And then we will

discuss Thomas Hunt Morgan's experiment with fruit flies and their mutations."

Uncle David took ten minutes to explain the trial's importance, how the entire country was watching, and how many people thought the trial pitted Darwin and evolution against the Bible and creation. "In actuality, the Scopes trial is about freedom to teach and to let students decide what they believe. Other than that, in my opinion, the trial is a sham. It doesn't mean much, just a way for people to discuss their differences."

Josh crossed his arms and shook his head. He'd read about the trial in Uncle David's newspapers, and he had a different opinion. But, of course, no one would listen to a thirteen-year-old boy. *Wait a moment...* He'd just remembered reading about the trial. Was he getting better?

"Josh, do you have something on your mind?" Uncle David grinned. "Perhaps we should hear from someone about to enter high school. Ladies and gentlemen, this is my niece and nephew, Abbigail and Joshua Hunter. Go ahead, Josh. What do you think?"

Josh straightened, his heart hammering his ribs. Talking in front of others was hard. At least, for him. He prayed his voice wouldn't crack. "Um, well, each teacher can't help but give more weight to either creation or to evolution, depending on what they believe. No one can be entirely fair."

The room, silent before, was now so tense Josh could hear breathing.

Uncle David's smile was kind. "Perhaps you're right." He circled his hand, indicating he wanted Josh to continue. "Do you believe evolution should *not* be taught?"

Josh shrugged. "I don't care." But Uncle David seemed to

want more, so he tried to choose his words carefully, struggling to remember things he'd heard his father say on the subject. "I think talking about different ideas is good. Letting the student weigh the evidence and decide for themselves is even better, something a good teacher would do."

"Give us an example, Josh."

An example? Didn't Uncle David know how hard it was to think on the spot like this? As if his mind was finally waking up, an idea came. "Maybe when on a test or a quiz. If the student disagrees with the teacher and puts real evidence on quizzes and tests for his argument, the answer should be accepted." He leaned his elbows on his knees and clasped his hands. "But if the teacher says evolution is the right answer, no matter the evidence the student gives, then it is not science and discovery any more, it's brainwashing—"

"But evolution is fact," insisted a student behind Josh. "Evolution is science. Not religion, like creation. Evolution is the correct answer on the test."

Josh shifted to look at him. "Studying creation is as scientific as studying geology or..." He turned to squint at the chart on the easel.

And then something happened in his head that hadn't happened for more than a month. The picture on the easel brought an encyclopedia entry to mind. "Or like studying Archaeopteryx."

The student behind him sputtered. "Churches and creation are religion. Scientists and evolution, fact. Religion is superstition and fairy tales."

Josh straightened and looked at the student. "Yes, listen to teachers and scientists." A heat built up in his chest that he'd never felt before. "But why am I not allowed an opinion, just because I go to church?"

The student stammered a moment, then said, "You only do what you're told in a church. I...Well...you're just a Bible thumper. What'dya know, anyway?"

"If you mean I believe the Bible, yes. God said in His Word that He created the world, and many people consider that an eye-witness account of the creation of the universe. But, think about this. If the Bible is true, then we should find some scientific, physical evidence for Noah's flood, which we do. We find flood evidence everywhere. We find sedimentary rock all over the planet. We find fossils of plants and animals buried quickly in those rock layers. We find polystrate fossils, like trees standing straight up crossing multiple layers of strata."

Josh gathered steam as he went, almost forgetting to be nervous, almost as if he was the professor. "Another event we can look for evidence on is the Tower of Babel. There is evidence that all our languages have common roots and that mankind spread out over the earth from one location in the Middle East. And, most importantly, was Jesus God, and did He walk this earth and rise from the dead? If the evidence supports these Biblical events, which it does, it is a safe bet the rest of the Bible is true, too."

A deep voice from the other side of the room brought the discussion to a halt. "What do you think, Dr. Hunter?"

Everyone looked at Professor Thomas. He lifted his eyebrows. "Do you think evolution should be taught along with creation?"

Josh turned to his uncle, who looked as if he didn't want to answer. But everyone in the room was waiting for his response. "I... You know I teach that creation theory is a myth."

His uncle rubbed his thumbs against his fingers. "But I believe that if the evidence points toward creation, then yes, creation must be taught."

Professor Thomas clicked his tongue and shook his head. "That's not science. It's not observable, not testable. It's religion. Faith. Fairy tales," he said, waving his hands dismissively

"But there *is* evidence!" Josh jumped up. "We just returned from the Doheny Expedition, where we found evidence of man and dinosaurs walking the earth at the same time—"

Professor Thomas sat up and tilted his head to the side, giving a warning with his eyes.

Abby grasped his arm. "Josh," she whispered. "He might hurt us."

Josh realized his mistake.

Before he could say anything, the student behind him grunted. "What do you know? You're just a stupid kid. Perhaps you're the missing link, fatso."

Josh fell into his seat as if he'd been slugged.

Abby gasped, then whispered, "Ignore him, Josh."

"That remark was completely uncalled for, Jenkins." Uncle David slapped his hand on the desk. "There is no room in education or science for name-calling. This club is an opportunity for scientific minds to learn from each other, not attack each other. Good manners first, or you're out of this class. Permanently."

Josh felt the tears coming. He sucked in deep breaths to calm his pounding heart, but that didn't help. He jumped to his feet and ran from the room, past the animal displays and through the double doors. Darting into a dark campus, he bumped into two men in trench coats and dark bowler hats. One of them grabbed his shoulder. "Sorry, boy."

Josh pulled away and was about to run when one of them said, "Say, you just came from the Biology Building, right?"

He nodded.

"You wouldn't happen to know if Dr. Hunter is in."

"He's there." Josh turned to go. "In his classroom, with his precious Darwin Club."

He ran all the way home, flung the front door open, and charged through the living room to his bedroom. He slammed his door shut with a satisfying smack.

He would never leave his bed again. Except to get the film, develop the pictures, and prove them all wrong.

CHAPTER FIVE
May 1925 - Same Day, Sunset
Colbey, Tennessee

Abby peered out the window into the darkening sky, trying to locate the bird that sang in front of Uncle David's house. Was it singing because the thunderstorm had passed? Other trees in the yard were bigger, but the bird seemed to like one of the smaller trees. Perhaps because the tree was closest to the house and farthest from the shadowy picket fence, flower gardens, and sidewalk. She opened the window and breathed in the fresh smell of storm-cleaned air and grass.

Josh would know the bird's species just by listening to its chirp. He might even know what kind of tree it sat in, as well as what the bird was saying. Abby would have smiled if she hadn't been so worried.

The bird stopped chirping.

Then Abby heard footsteps coming up the walk.

At the sound of a knock, she rushed to the front door. She opened it, letting in the fresh, moist air. "Miss Emma. Thank you for coming…I didn't know who else to talk to."

"I'm glad you called." Miss Emma shook out her umbrella before stepping inside and sliding it into the umbrella stand.

Abby rubbed her temples, trying to hold back tears. "I'm sorry, but I can't find Uncle David. I tried calling his office, and no one answered. He hasn't come home from the Darwin Club meeting yet."

"He's probably talking with students." Miss Emma took off her red gloves. "What's wrong with Josh?"

"He locked himself in his room and hasn't come out since he left the meeting. I can hear him crying, but he won't answer me." Josh would be mad at her for calling a grownup, but she didn't care. He'd never acted this way before. "One of the students called him fat. Okay, so Josh is kinda out of shape and kinda sloppy with his clothes, but to call him fatso… That was just mean."

Miss Emma's eyes narrowed. "Which bedroom is his?"

Abby wiped her tears away and led her through the living room, weaving around Uncle David's books and fossil collections.

Footsteps paused outside Josh's door. Two people, by the sound of the steps, probably Abby and Uncle David. A moment later, he heard Abby's soft knock. "Josh, it's me. Miss Emma's here. She… Josh, please. Can we talk?"

"Go away."

"Josh, please come out." Miss Emma's voice was gentle. "I'm…worried about your Uncle David. He's gone missing."

Missing? He swiped at his swollen eyes with the back of his hand.

"I'm about to fix something to eat. If your Uncle David isn't home by the time we finish, we'll go search for him. I hope you'll join me and Abby."

Josh didn't respond, but five minutes later, when the smell of sizzling bacon and eggs became more than he could resist, Josh slipped from his bed and quietly opened the door.

"Oh, no," Miss Emma was saying. "Not the toaster. That machine makes bread taste terrible. Put it in a pan on the stove with butter. It's the only way to heat bread."

"That's what I keep telling the menfolk," Abby said, "But Uncle David says" —she imitated his voice—"We need to keep up with technology, so use the toaster, girl."

Josh stepped into the kitchen as Miss Emma pulled three plates from the cabinet. She set them on the countertop and smiled at him.

"Hello, Josh. Dinner's almost ready." She acted as if she'd never doubted he'd join them. "I didn't see anything to drink in the icebox, but I did find a bucket of oranges. Can you squeeze some juice for us?"

"I'm not going to eat."

Miss Emma put her hands on her hips. "Fiddle faddle. A person must keep up her—or his—energy." She nodded at

Abby. "Right, Abby?"

His sister grinned.

Josh set an orange on the cutting board, sliced it in half, then pressed it into the cone of the juicer, forcing juice from the pulp. As he worked, he caught his reflection in a nearby window. He looked as bad as he felt, like wilted lettuce. If only he could take a pill that would make him happy again. Or bring his mom and dad back.

"I need eggs and bacon. Let's eat," Miss Emma said as she picked up the skillet and dumped scrambled eggs onto three plates.

They finished setting the table, sat, and said grace. Josh took a few bites, then a sip of orange juice he'd just squeezed. He felt better already.

"So, what happened to the boy?" Miss Emma asked, then took a bite of eggs. "The one that was so rude?"

"After Josh left, Uncle David said the boy—Jenkins, I think his name was—might consider a written apology, and that he should remember the day a thirteen-year-old got the better of him. And when Jenkins tried to argue, Uncle David kicked the boy out of the club."

Miss Emma reached over and gripped his shoulder. "We're all different, Josh. Each of us has a size and shape that's just right for us. Not one person looks like another. Even twins look a little different. But some people try to fit everyone into a mold, and when people don't fit their mold, they say mean things, things that aren't always true."

Josh took another sip of orange juice. "It's not that." He wiped his lips on his sleeve.

Miss Emma slipped out of her chair and knelt beside him. "You miss your parents?"

Had she read his mind? He squeezed his eyelids tight to stop the tears from coming.

Miss Emma patted his back. "I lost my mother when I was your age. I still miss her." Her sigh was so sad, so honest. "I know what it's like to lose a parent. You two lost both of your parents. I can't begin to imagine your pain, but I hurt for you."

The telephone rang, and all three of them jumped. Josh grabbed his heart. Why was he so jumpy all of a sudden?

"I don't know if I'll ever get used to that sound. Even in the office, it scares me." Miss Emma walked around the opposite wall that separated the kitchen and dining room from the front door and living room, and they heard her pull the earpiece from the side of the phone box. "Professor David Hunter's residence," she said loudly. After a second, she said, "Hello, Fred."

Josh looked over his shoulder at his uncle's fiancée. He couldn't hear the person on the other end of the phone line, but whatever Fred said, it made Miss Emma sound like she was frowning. "No, he doesn't have a cousin. Are you sure?"

He and Abby exchanged questioning glances.

"No," Miss Emma went on. "I don't mean to imply that you don't know what you're doing, but it seems strange—"

After a long moment, she set the receiver back on the cradle. She walked around the corner and looked at Abby and Josh. "That was the drugstore. Someone claiming to be David's cousin picked up a pack of pictures after we turned in the film yesterday." She stepped to the sink and started the water, dropped in soap, and set the skillet in the suds. "David turned in the film from our picnic and someone else paid for the pictures and took them. Very strange."

Miss Emma scrubbed the grease and egg residue from the cast-iron skillet and dried it. "We have to wash and dry iron pans quickly," she said, "to keep them from rusting." Her brow furrowed. "Why would someone else pick up our pictures?"

"I know why." Abby's face was white. "They're looking for our film. They think we had that film processed."

Josh held his breath. Was she going to tell Miss Abby about the film? That had to be a secret, or it might get out where they'd hidden it! Then the mobsters might get to it before they could retrieve it!

Abby gasped when she realized her mistake.

But Miss Emma didn't seem to notice. Instead, she seemed to be listening to something else.

Footsteps. Then a shadow passed across the small kitchen window.

Miss Emma tilted her head. "Sounds like David is back."

Josh felt Abby's nails dig into his arm. "The bird stopped chirping out front."

Josh frowned. "Those footsteps came from the side of the house—"

Abby finished his sentence. "And Uncle David only uses the front door."

"Uncle David took his car to the school today, since he had to take one of his tortoise shells for display."

He and Abby looked at each other. Something was wrong.

"Listen to you two." Emma laughed. "Relax, it's nothing." Despite her brave words, her voice shook. She peered through the window, but the sun had set, and the view was black.

Heavy footsteps crunched in the gravel beside the house,

and the gate squeaked open. Everyone froze. Miss Emma dropped the cup she was washing into the suds, then quickly wiped the soap off her hands. "Um…I'm going to check it out. Stay here."

She tiptoed, skillet in one hand, out of the kitchen, down the hall, past the bedrooms, and out of sight to the back door.

Abby looked as if she was about to say something, when Josh heard a loud bonk, then thud.

"Miss Emma!" Abby called.

They sprinted out of the kitchen, down the hall, and to the open back door, where they slid to a stop. Josh pushed the switch to turn on the electric light.

Miss Emma stood over a limp form on the back porch. She dropped the skillet and knelt beside the body. "Oh, David, I'm so sorry! Are you all right?"

He groaned. "No, I'm not all right."

"I'm so sorry. I thought you were after the kids."

Abby rushed to his side, and Josh leaned down, ready to help lift his uncle to the hospital.

"Who did you think I was?" He sat up and rubbed his neck. "The boogeyman? Al Capone?"

"Well, yes…" Miss Emma glanced between Josh and Abby. "We got a strange phone call that set us all on edge."

Miss Emma took one of Uncle David's hands, and Josh took the other, and they lifted him to his feet.

"Why didn't you use the front door?" Abby asked.

"Normally, I do." He swayed. "But the front door was wide open, so I went around back, in case a burglar was in the house. Didn't want him banging me on the head with a frying pan. I thought I'd surprise him."

Josh watched Miss Emma and Abby's eyes meet. They

spoke at the same time. "The door was closed." They stared through the open doorway, obviously thinking the same thing he was thinking. Someone was inside the house.

Miss Emma picked up the skillet.

CHAPTER SIX
May, 1925 - Five Heartbeats Later
Colbey, Tennessee

Josh swallowed hard. He wanted to run away so badly, he could almost feel his legs moving toward the alley.

But he needed to protect Abby, and now Uncle David and Miss Emma. Instead of running, he gritted his teeth, clamped his jaw, and took a step inside.

Uncle David whispered, "Josh, stop."

Josh turned to see he held up a finger, indicating they should wait.

Uncle David took the skillet from Miss Emma's hand and

put his finger to his lips. "Stay behind me."

Josh took a deep breath and followed his uncle.

The others fell in line behind him.

Uncle David started into the house, the skillet held high. He stopped in the middle of the hallway. They all stopped.

Uncle David tilted his head. They all tilted their heads.

Someone was in Josh's room. The sound reminded him of when his mother rummaged through her purse. It was *his* bag being rummaged through. Then his dresser drawer pulled out.

Someone was after the film. He was sure of it.

He was tempted to take the skillet from Uncle David and rush into the room. Sometimes being mad helped him be brave.

He shared a quick, knowing look with Abby.

Uncle David peered around the corner of the door, then slipped to the other side. Josh struggled to comprehend that someone, possibly a killer, was inside his room, going through his things. Was it Professor Thomas?

Josh moved to stand in front of his sister. His first responsibility was to protect her. The rustling in the room stopped. When he could no longer hold his breath, Josh let it out, painfully aware his breathing was too loud.

Uncle David stretched high, holding the frying pan above his head with both hands, ready to whack the intruder when he or she exited the bedroom.

The rustling was replaced by the sound of furniture being moved and then another familiar noise. The intruder was opening the window!

Uncle David yelled, "Stop!" He threw the door wide open and darted into the dark room.

Josh followed, right on his heels.

His uncle was a mere shadow moving toward the window, but the trespasser was half inside the room and half outside, his leg and shoulder illuminated by moonlight.

Uncle David lunged forward and with one hand, grabbed the man, yanking him back inside the room.

The burglar slammed against the dresser. He groaned.

A loud click, and the overhead light blinded him. Josh held up an arm to shield his eyes from the dazzling bulb.

The burglar grunted and stood. Although Josh could barely see him through his light-blinded vision, he yelled, "Stop him!"

Josh's uncle, who still held the frying pan in his hand, struggled to stand as well, but the burglar shoved him on his back.

The burglar's sweaty face came into focus. His long hair was combed over a bald spot. Josh reached for anything he could get his hands on. His fingers wrapped around his bag. He swung directly at the crown of the intruder's head. The burglar only winced.

The stranger dashed for the door, but Abby and Emma blocked his exit.

The man's brown vest was half off, and his beige pants slipped below his ample gut. He pulled his vest tight, hitched up his britches, then swung his fist.

Miss Emma ducked.

The man threw his left fist. A sickening *smack* filled the room, along with a scream as Abby flew into the hallway. The burglar pushed past Miss Emma, knocking her to the ground.

Abby scrambled to her feet and launched herself at the

intruder. Never in his life had he heard such an angry, vicious yell from his sister. Or from his own throat. How dare he attack Abby?

The man flung Abby aside like a ragdoll and ran out the front door before Josh could reach him.

Uncle David tried to stand again but fell back down. He tried again, and managed to make it to Abby's side. "You okay? Let me see…"

Miss Emma stood in the doorway, holding her arm. "Josh? Are you okay?"

He nodded, and he and Uncle David helped his sister up. Her eye was already swelling shut.

"Did you get him, Josh?" She touched her eyelid and winced.

Uncle David looked into Abby's eyes, then checked Miss Emma's arm, then asked Josh if he was okay.

"I'm all right."

"Good, I'm going after him." Uncle David started down the hall, but Miss Emma stopped him.

"Please, David, just call the police. Please stay with us."

He looked for a moment down the hall toward the door, but then nodded. "I'll call."

Josh helped everyone hobble to the front room, his mind racing. That man was one more proof that their parents' deaths were not accidental. The intruder had been looking for the film. Josh was sure.

He was disappointed the man wasn't Professor Thomas, but that simply meant the professor had help. More than one bad guy was involved in this mess to find the film, just like in Arizona at the falls.

CHAPTER SEVEN
May, 1925 - Thirty Minutes Later
Colbey, Tennessee

Josh dug ice out of the icebox, wrapped it in cloth, and took the bundle to Abby in the front room. As he passed Uncle David, who was on the couch rigging a sling for Miss Emma's arm, he asked, "Will you need ice, too?"

"No," she said, then looked at Uncle David. "And like I said a minute ago, I don't need a doctor."

"We'll have a doctor look at it in the morning," Uncle David said, finishing the knot and adjusting the cloth to fit her arm.

Josh passed the coffee table and leaned over Abby. He studied her eye. "It's swollen, but not turning black yet."

She touched her brow. "It feels strange. Almost like it's not my eye. Should have given the burglar a shiner, too."

"Can you see okay?"

"Yep. It's not going to turn black, is it? I'll be so disappointed if it doesn't turn black"

Josh shook his head and sagged into the chair beside Abby. To distract himself from his troubles, he studied the massive tortoise shell that hung above the fireplace, the second shell normally right next to it was at the school. The shell display was surrounded by fragments of flat stone. Each rock contained an imprint of a plant, dating back—or so his uncle said—millions of years.

A short couch and four padded chairs lined the walls of the small living room, each with a bookshelf next to it. The radio next to the piano played a soothing Beethoven piano concerto. Well, maybe it was Beethoven. Josh wasn't positive. He'd continued to have trouble remembering such easy details.

The fireplace crackled, warm against his skin.

Uncle David sat on the edge of the couch beside Miss Emma.

"How's your head?" Miss Emma asked.

"Fine, except I can still taste the sour chalk of the aspirin tablet. Ugh." He helped her adjust her arm. "How's that feel?"

She settled her elbow into the cloth. "Peachy, thanks." She relaxed against the couch back.

A knock at the door made them all jump.

"It's okay," Uncle David said. "I'm sure it's just the police finishing up." He went and opened the door a crack, then swung it wide.

The police officer brushed his thick mustache. "We dusted for fingerprints and will take them back to the office. Too many footprints to make sense of anything. Oh, and we did find this." He held out a small packet. "Pictures. You must have dropped them."

Uncle David took the photos, thanked the officer, and wished him a good evening. He shut the door, crossed the room to sit by Miss Emma, and opened the pictures. "They're of our picnic."

Abby sighed. "I can't believe they found us." Her voice was soft, and Uncle David and Miss Emma didn't seem to notice.

"What did you think would happen?" Josh turned to her and crossed his arms. "Of course they would track us to Uncle David's place. We live with our only relative."

"They're looking for the film." Abby chewed at her lip for a moment before turning to her uncle. "Uncle David, do you mind if we borrow your car?"

"What?" He jerked his head toward her, still holding a picture in midair. "Why? Where are you going?"

"Arizona," Abby said. "But not for long. We'd come right back."

Josh hadn't wanted to tell anyone, but now that Uncle David had been attacked, Miss Emma injured, and especially Abby hurt, he needed to employ help.

"Sorry, Josh," Abby said, adjusting the ice bag. "I didn't mean to tell…" She fell silent.

"Arizona is some long ways away. You want to see your parent's graves?"

"No, well, yes, I would like to go back to see my parents."

Josh swallowed the lump growing in his throat. "But there's more, and… That guy wasn't just here robbing the house. We know what he was looking for."

Except for the crickets which sung to the quiet night, and the sound of water dripping from the roof, the room was silent.

Josh whispered. "You must keep this secret."

Uncle David exchanged glances with Miss Emma. He set the pictures on the coffee tabled and leaned back, crossing one leg over his knee. "Go ahead, Josh."

"In Arizona, Abby and I found tracks. Dinosaur tracks, and human footprints, side by side."

Uncle David's eyes widened and he leaned forward again. "You what?"

"We found the tracks and took pictures," Abby shouted, as if trying to convince Uncle David. "We have proof."

"Men came with crowbars and pickaxes while we were there. They broke up the evidence. I snapped pictures of it, but we were spotted. We got away, but they shot at us."

"Shot at us," Abby repeated.

"We…" He hesitated. This was the big secret. The location of the film. This information would hurt people if it got into the wrong hands. "We stashed the film in Arizona and found Mom and Dad. They drove us to a hotel. Mom and Dad returned to the site the next day, but that was when…" Josh swallowed the pain and made himself say the words. "That's when they were hit. And died."

Abby's sniffling brought him to a halt, and he put his hand on her back. Miss Emma crossed the room. She wrapped an arm around Abby and squeezed Josh's shoulder. He leaned into her embrace.

"Josh, should we tell them about...*him*?"

The relief of giving his troubles to someone else for a moment pushed Josh on. "Professor Thomas was one of the men who destroyed the evidence."

"Thomas Thomas? From Colbey? He was in Arizona?"

Josh and Abby nodded.

Uncle David leaned back and brought his hand up to his chin, thinking. Finally, he said, "I've never liked him. Even when we were in school together."

"David!" Miss Emma whispered.

"You don't believe them? He was always up to no good."

Miss Emma gave him a stern look. "I didn't say that. But be nice."

Abby said in a doleful voice, "When the police turned over the things in the car, all the stuff was there. Everything but the camera."

Uncle David didn't move. His eyes, however, showed intense interest. "You mean the one you used to photograph the footprints?"

Josh gave the nearby globe a spin. "Yes, and they know the film was gone. They're looking for the photographs we took of them destroying the human tracks."

Uncle David jumped to his feet and paced near the front door. "And they thought we were developing them, so they tried to steal them from Fred at the drug store?"

Josh spun the world in circles again. This was getting them nowhere. With his memory gone—or shaky, at best—and with everyone injured, except him... And with Mom and Dad dead, and no way to get to Arizona, he simply didn't have any options.

Uncle David grabbed his head. "Oh no. No! I forgot," he shouted as he crossed the room and reached over Josh. He snatched a box from over the mantel and returned to the couch. Miss Emma scooted close beside him.

He pulled out an envelope, slipped a piece of paper from inside, and unfolded a page. Josh could see writing through the paper. Uncle David studied the letter for about a minute.

Finally, he spoke. "About a week after Josh and Abby's parents died, I received a note in the mail. I didn't know what it meant. It was...odd."

After clearing his throat, he read the letter aloud.

David,

The mob wants the negatives of our recent finds. The mob is always paid by someone and we're not sure who is paying them. They're destroying evidence of archeological records at Havasupai Falls. Not sure why. I will call when I can. I may need your help. Please consider coming to Arizona to pick up the children.

Peter

Dad had written to Uncle David shortly before he and mom were killed.

Uncle David looked up. "I received this the day after you

came, and I meant to ask what it was about."

Abby sniffed.

Josh glanced at his sister. Her lip quivered.

Abby got up from her chair and walked over to Miss Emma, who patted the cushion beside her. Abby slid next to her and Miss Emma put her arm around her.

Abby reached out and, with her finger, traced Dad's handwriting.

Josh swallowed the lump in his throat and blinked back tears.

Uncle David frowned. "I guess those are the tracks you shot? The mob wants *the negatives*?"

"The film negatives." Josh said, testing his voice, which was surprisingly strong. "When you take a picture with a camera, the image is imprinted on the film. It's called a negative."

Uncle David winked. "I know what negatives and film are." He took a shuddering breath. "But... Your parents were killed because of film negatives? I don't understand." He shook his head. "Why didn't the two of you tell me about what happened in Arizona earlier?"

"We didn't think anyone would believe us," Abby said.

Josh spun the globe again, thinking. "I'm sorry. I thought not telling you would protect everyone."

"I need to talk with Emma for a moment," Uncle David said. "Will you two be okay by yourselves for a bit?"

Josh shrugged, but Abby said, "sure."

The moment the adults left the room and disappeared behind the wall separating the front room and kitchen, Abby flipped around, putting the ice bag back on her eye. "Do you think they believe us?"

"I bet that's what they're discussing right now."

"Yeah, but—" Abby snapped her mouth shut midsentence. "Come on, I think we can hear them." She slipped off the couch and paused at the arch leading into the kitchen. Josh joined her, leaning his back against the wall and tilting his head toward the opening.

"They're hurting inside, David. We've got to do something."

"What do you suggest?" he asked.

"You may not like my idea." She sighed. "I'm sure you're not going to like it."

"You mean go to Arizona? I can't just—"

"This is 1925, not 1900! The airplane! You can go after class Friday and be back Monday. Surely Father will cover your class for you if you're gone longer. Just call me."

"Your father will object. I have papers to grade."

She laughed. "Let me take care of Father."

"I'm afraid leaving's not that simple." Josh heard Uncle David tapping the counter with silverware. "In my office tonight, before I came home—"

Her low voice held a note of warning. "I know you work hard, too hard, but coming home this late…Josh really needed you tonight."

"Two men from Dayton, Tennessee, came to the classroom after the club meeting. They said they're looking for scientists to testify in the Scopes Trial and asked me to be an expert witness to help prove evolution before a judge."

"Prove evolution? In court?"

"The defense wants to use scientists to show that the law banning evolution from the classroom is silly and unjust."

"What did you tell them?"

"Free speech must prevail. I told them yes."

Abby glanced at Josh, her eyes wide.

He sighed and shook his head.

Uncle David added, "The trial is in July."

"That's incredible, David. I'm so happy for you. This is great for your career..." She paused.

"But?"

"You have time to go to Arizona, if you fly. Remember, Fred owes you a big favor." The smile returned to her voice. "You can balance both career and family." She was quiet for a moment. "There may be nothing to the kids' worries. The car accident was probably just that, an accident. But you need to help them put their minds at ease."

Josh leaned forward, listening carefully to every word.

"I suppose I could call Fred tomorrow and ask him if the airplane is flight-ready."

Josh's heart beat faster. An airplane?

Miss Emma clapped. "Oh, how I wish I could go with you."

"I wish you could go with us, too." He coughed. "Just a quick flight from Nashville to Arizona. No problem."

"Posh. Of course, it's not a problem. People fly every day across this country. Just last month the flight from Paris to New York was showing movies. Movies! On a plane!"

"But the plane Fred lets me fly has two cockpits, both un-covered."

"You'll make the flight work."

Abby stared at Josh, her mouth wide open, and then, throwing the ice bag to the side, she rushed into the kitchen. "You mean we're going on an airplane ride?"

Josh heard his uncle laugh. "Looks like it! You shouldn't

be listening around corners."

Josh followed his sister into the kitchen. "Uncle David, I didn't know you're a pilot."

His uncle smiled. "There's a lot you two don't know about me."

Miss Emma held out her hand to Uncle David, and he handed over Dad's letter. "Do you mind if I show this to my father? Maybe he'll know who is paying the mob within the archeology community. He knows a lot of professors across the country."

"Just be careful." Uncle David rubbed the back of his neck. He winced. "Remember the intruder? Whoever is behind finding this film, they're serious."

CHAPTER EIGHT
May, 1925 - The Next Morning, Saturday
On the Road to Nashville

In the backseat behind Uncle David, Abby tapped her foot on the floor of the car and talked over the rumble of the engine. She couldn't help herself. Miss Emma wasn't here to keep her company since she'd promised to grade papers and talk to her father about the intruder.

"The steering wheel's just a round circle made of Cherrywood, connected to a pole, and when you turn the wheel, it cranks on the axle and turns the tires?"

Josh, in the front passenger seat, turned to her and nodded. "That's about right."

Uncle David kept his focus on the road, but she wanted him to talk, too. "Four pedals, Uncle David?"

He just nodded, then slowed, punched a pedal down, then shifted gears with the stick on his right. The car hit a pothole and dipped, jarring the cabin. She enjoyed bouncing on the back seat.

She sat back up and checked the speedometer. Thirty miles per hour, which was sad, since the car could go sixty. Why not use all the speed you could get? Uncle David was safe, for sure, but too safe. The engine roared, even at these speeds. Imagine pushing the accelerator to the floor. How loud would it be, then?

"Congress has a committee talking about fixing these roads now," Josh said, looking first to Uncle David, then including her in the conversation by glancing her way.

The tall trees on each side of the road seemed to speed by, but the wind from the open windows didn't do much to cool down the hot spring day. She smelled freshly mown grass as they passed a field.

Even though they'd gotten a late start on the day and she was starving, she couldn't wait before she climbed into an airplane for the first time. And they still had an hour left on the road.

She turned to glance behind them again. The black Model T was still following them. He'd been behind them since Colbey. She could just make out a man with a stern face.

"You know how car companies promote auto trails from town to town, right?" Josh asked.

She turned back to the front.

Uncle David nodded but kept his eye on the road.

"I don't know what you're talking about, Josh," she said.

"Then states took roads and turned them into something they call highways, giving them numbers. But the Senate committee is meeting today. I just read the report in the papers. They want roads constructed across America just like this one to make travel easier for everyone."

The car rattled and the windows shook. Abby grabbed the seat. The springs creaked as she bounced, and she smiled. Bumps were great!

"Washboard road." Josh pointed through the window. "They didn't grade it correctly. If the graders had built the crown in the center of the road…"

He talked on and on about how to construct the perfect road, and Abby tuned him out. She leaned her head out the window, and couldn't hear the voices, only the roar of the wind.

When she pulled her head back inside, Josh was saying, "Everything points to creation, like with the human and dinosaur footprints side by side. You have to twist what you find to fit evolution's ideas, like saying that the tracks didn't exist, or that the ground softened one million years later and humans walked over it again."

Uncle David tapped the steering wheel with both thumbs. "Everyone who observed the past is dead, evolution is the best guess."

"Just a guess?" Abby said, leaning between the two front seats.

Uncle David sighed and cleared his throat. "It's what the evidence shows."

He slowed the car, and pulled into a restaurant's parking lot. "We'll eat here, then be at the airport in fifteen minutes."

Abby visited the outhouse behind the building and walked past four cars—Uncle David's blue car, one cream-and-red car, one brown like shoe leather, and near the front door, a red car that she decided she would buy someday and drive to church every Sunday. She paused, glanced around for the Model T, but it seemed they'd lost him.

She pushed open the door, and a tiny catch over the door, attached to a bell, rang to announce visitors. She walked through, into a gift shop, then into the restaurant to the right.

A single aisle with tables on either side stretched the length of the building. She saw Josh and Uncle David by a window. They leaned close in a heated debate. She sat, and they clamped their mouths shut.

"What's wrong? Abby asked.

"Nothing." Josh glowered at his uncle, who heaved a sigh and rubbed his hands together.

"Josh thinks we should tell you, so I will." He rested his forearms on the table, leaned close and spoke just above a whisper. "We're being followed."

"The black Model T?" She retied her ponytail. "I haven't seen him for about twenty minutes.

Josh grinned and said as statement instead of a question, "Oh, so you already know about the car."

"It's been following us since Colbey. I thought it might be the police." She basked in their surprised expressions, until Uncle David frowned.

He glanced at the passing waitress, and then focused on Abby. "Please tell me whenever you notice unusual or suspicious activities, okay?"

"I wasn't sure he was following us. But the driver looks like a hardboiled criminal." She pointed to Josh's hat. "We're eating."

Josh snatched his newsboy cap from his head and slipped it under his leg. "I haven't seen him up close. But I wouldn't be surprised if it was the same guy who broke into the house."

She said, "Maybe he's a detective?"

Uncle David shook his head. "I don't know. More likely, he's the intruder."

"Do you think we lost him?"

"We're going to continue on." Uncle David adjusted his tie and took off his suit jacket. "And we'll reach our destination, safe and sound." He put on his spectacles and studied the menu. "But keep your eyes open." He looked at them over the top of the menu. "Wide open."

In unison, Abby and Josh sat tall, their eyes wide and their heads erect.

Uncle David laughed. "Let's see how long you can go without blinking." He watched the waitress go by again. "Wow, this place certainly isn't Mack's back home. When is she going to take our order? I'm starved." He pushed back his chair. "I need to use the restroom. If she comes over, order me a hamburger, will you?" He snatched a newspaper from an empty table and walked out the front door.

The waitress stepped up and took their drink order.

The radio started playing an orchestrated version of *Tea for Two*, and Abby noticed everyone in the restaurant spoke louder to be heard over the music. She nudged Josh's leg with her foot, placed her elbows on the table and rested her chin on her folded hands.

"Josh," she whispered, "he left because he thinks we're safe. I know God will protect us, but I sure don't feel that way right now."

"God didn't keep Mom and Dad safe."

She stared at him. Where did that come from? "How can you say such a thing?"

The waitress set two root beers in front of them and left.

"You're right." Josh rubbed his thumb across the table edge. "I...I shouldn't blame God for that."

"Remember what Dad said about Adam and Eve? God didn't want them to eat the tree's fruit, but they did anyway. God didn't want someone to kill Mom and Dad, but they did it anyway."

"Maybe it was an accident, like the sheriff in Arizona says."

"You know better than that—" She froze. "Josh, he's here." She pointed at the window. "The man who broke into our house." They watched the car roll to a stop, and he opened the door, then stepped out. He wore a wrinkled suit instead of slacks and a shirt like before, but there was no doubt. He was the intruder. He tossed something inside the Model T, then paused at Uncle David's car. Then he started inside.

Josh gasped. "It *is* him."

"He's coming into the restaurant. Should we run?" Abby slid against the wall.

"Isn't he afraid we'll recognize him?"

"Maybe he doesn't care. I mean, what can we do to him? Only the Colbey police are looking for him, and they can't get here any time soon."

When the man stepped inside the restaurant, he stopped and scanned the room. But he pretended not to notice them. Without removing his hat, he crossed the tile floor and walked straight down the aisle.

He was coming close. Abby squeezed closer to the window. So close now.

He didn't look at them. He walked past.

He sat in a booth with his back to them.

"He knows we're here." Abby gripped the edge of her seat. "And he's watching Uncle David's car."

"I know." Josh picked up his root beer and took a sip. His hands were shaking.

"How can you drink at a time like this?"

"I'm thirsty." He took another drink. "And hungry. Besides, he's not going to hurt us. Not here in the open. He may not even be following us. Just traveling back to whoever hired him."

She shook her head. Josh was just ignoring the problem, like he always did when he didn't have a plan. What she needed was something to show who this man was, and who paid him. Then they'd be getting somewhere. She could encourage Uncle David to walk over and force the information out of the man. Or she could do a little spying.

She chose spying.

"Josh, watch him." She scooted away from the window toward the aisle. "Make sure he doesn't go out to his car."

He choked on the root beer. "Abby, how am I supposed to stop him? Don't tell me you're going to... No, you can't."

"He can't see his car from where he's sitting. Just don't let him catch me in it."

"Uncle David expects you to stay here! Besides, breaking into that guy's car is illegal!"

"So is breaking into a house and giving a girl a black eye. This is the only way." She slipped from the booth and walked like a ballet dancer straight past the tables and into the gift shop. One eye on the man, she opened the front door just a crack so that it didn't catch the bell. She squeezed out the front door. If the lady at the cash register thought Abby was strange, she didn't say anything.

She tried to look casual as she walked between the Model T and another car that had just pulled in, but her pounding heart beat so loudly she was sure the whole world could hear it.

The car window was open a few inches. She reached inside and tugged on the latch. The door opened.

Leaving it open, she slipped inside and quickly searched the vehicle. A leather briefcase sat on the passenger-side floor.

Abby reached for it, but then the bell over the restaurant door jingled. If she were caught going through the guy's car...

She scrambled into the car, shut the door behind her, and dove over the seat and into the back. She peered over the back-door window and watched an elderly man help his crippled wife through the door.

She almost laughed with relief. She rubbed her sweaty hands on her pants and reached over the seat for the briefcase. She'd pull it into the back seat, where she felt most protected from roving eyes.

The bell rang again. She glanced up. Someone shoved the restaurant door open, nearly knocking the old woman to the ground. Abby sucked in a breath. Oh, no! The man who'd been following them was already leaving the restaurant.

Abby let go of the briefcase and slipped under the back seat. She squeezed against the backseat floor and lay perfectly still.

Boots crunched against gravel, closer, closer.

The driver's door opened. She curled against the floor. *Please, God, don't let him look in the back seat.*

She tried to think of a plan of escape in case he started to drive away—and came up blank. She squeezed her eyes shut and prayed he wouldn't find her. The car shuddered when he dropped into the seat. And then she heard a snap, as if the briefcase was being opened, followed by an unscrewing sound of metal, then several gulps and a loud *ahhhh*.

He was drinking! She recognized the sounds and smells from some of the men on archeological digs.

He belched. *Disgusting.*

After a moment, she heard the scratch of a match, then a flare, and the smell of cigar smoke drifted into the back of the car.

Oh please, don't drive off...please!

He puffed for a while, until the smoke tickled Abby's nose. *Don't sneeze!*

Why, when she told herself something, that was the one thing she *had* to do? She pressed her finger under her nose.

Finally, the seat shook again, the door opened and slammed, and the sound of boots on gravel drifted away. The bell rang, and she chanced a glance. Through the window, she saw him walking back to his table.

Abby nearly giggled with relief.

Wait. Had he taken the briefcase with him?

She peeked over the seat. Still there. With trembling hands, she pulled the briefcase to the back and opened it. A flap on the side dropped open, revealing two flasks. Whiskey! Drinking alcohol of any kind had been illegal ever since Prohibition became the law in 1920.

She snapped the side flap closed and opened the briefcase.

"Applesauce, he has a gun!" She pulled back as if there was a rattlesnake in the bag.

She shivered. The man meant business.

Beneath the gun, she found dozens of receipts from hotels, gas stations, diners, and cafes. Odd. They mostly were businesses in Colbey.

She shuffled through the pile until she came to the bottom and an envelope made out to her uncle in her father's handwriting. Why would he have this? She pulled the sheet from the envelope. The hair on her arms prickled. It was the note Uncle David had read to them.

She folded the letter and shoved it in her pocket. The mobster had no right to it. But she left the envelope, so he'd think he still had the note.

She stuffed the receipts back into the briefcase, laid the heavy gun back on top, and heaved the bag to the front. She pushed it to the floor and tumbled into the front seat, smack-

ing the springs hard.

Rubbing her ribs, she struggled for breath. After counting to twenty, she sat up and set the briefcase on the floor, exactly where she'd found it.

The door handle was hard to turn, but the lever finally released, and the door swung wide. She slipped off the seat, shut the door and hurried across the lot.

Again, she squeezed through the café door without making the bell ring and checked on the man. To her relief, he was sitting with his back to her again.

But then she heard Uncle David's voice from behind and jumped. "Abby, what are you doing?"

She spun around, about to say she was looking at the postcards on the counter. But that was a lie. Instead, she said, "He's here."

He leaned down and whispered, "Where?"

She pointed. "He's the one talking with the waitress."

Her uncle put his hand on her back. "C'mon, let's go sit down."

"We can ditch him! I'll grab Josh, and we'll take off."

He shook his head. "Good thinking, but he's obviously sure we don't recognize him. We don't want him to know we know."

Uncle David thought for a moment, then crossed to the woman behind the cash register. "Do you happen to have a phone? I need to call the police."

"Dear, there's not a phone within five miles."

Abby followed Uncle David back to their table.

"Abby!" Josh's eyes were wild. He leaped to his feet. "I thought he was going to drive away with you."

"What?" Uncle David sat across from them, a frown on

his face.

Abby sat and slid closer to the window, and Josh settled next to her.

"I just watched him walk by," Josh said, his eyes bright with unshed tears. "He just walked by, and I did nothing."

"What?" Uncle David looked confused.

"I'm the worst brother in the world." Josh took her hands, which surprised her. He rarely even hugged her. "I promise you, Abby, I will protect you. Forever. I'll never let that happen again. I was just so scared."

"It's okay, Josh. I can look after myself." The earnest fervor in his eyes broke her resolve, and she said, "Thanks. You do a good job looking after me. And hey, look what I found." She pulled the note from her pocket and handed it to Josh.

Uncle David glanced over the top of the page. "Where did you get this? Miss Emma had it to show her father."

She looked at the Model T. Then back to Uncle David.

He followed her gaze to the intruder's car, then back to her.

The full weight of his gaze pressed down on her like a steam locomotive. She was more afraid now than she'd been while trapped in the car. She slowly turned her head and aimed her chin at the Model T.

"You didn't."

The anger in his voice made her cringe.

"Please tell me you didn't."

She bit her bottom lip.

"You did."

He blew out a long breath, and then surprised her with a chuckle. But his laughter didn't last long. "Don't...ever...do that...again." He shook his finger at her.

Abby ducked her head. "I'll try not to."

He held out his hand. "Let me see that note."

When he took the page, he didn't read it. Instead, he folded the paper and tapped the corner against the table. "If they got this letter, Miss Emma may be in trouble. We should find a phone, call the police, and get back to Colbey to see if she's okay."

He kept tapping the letter on the table, and the music stopped, so she could hear the *tick tick tick* sound he made. Finally, he straightened. "Josh, you're an inspiration. You've been a good brother, and have protected Abby. But up to this point, I've been a pretty useless uncle. Time to change that."

Uncle David stood and tugged on the lapel of his jacket so that his wide shoulders were prominent. Handing Josh the letter, he said, "Stay here."

Uncle David marched to the intruder's table. He looked down at the older man, his firm jaw and fiery eyes pronounced. She heard her uncle clearly.

"Look, you. You barge into my home, hurt my family, and now follow us. I don't like that. Not one bit. I'm telling you right now, you won't get away with this. So don't make it worse. Stop following us. Tell whoever is hiring you to back off. Leave us alone. Or the police will find you, then him, and your lives in jail will be miserable. Got it?"

The man glared back at him. "Don't know what you're talking about, Mister."

"When the police come here in a few moments and match your fingerprints with the intruder's, you'll be singing a different tune."

The man jumped to his feet, stood directly next to her uncle, but the intruder looked small. "All right, you. I don't take orders from professors. And if anyone's going to be singing tunes, it's you. You don't know the trouble them kids have gotten you into. My advice? Turn around, drive home, and stay outta this." He set his hands on his hips. "After giving me the pictures them kids took."

Would his uncle do what the man asked?

Uncle David just looked at the intruder.

"Well?" the man finally asked. "What are you looking at me like that for?"

"Just imagining what you will look like in black and white prison stripes."

With face red and shaking fists, the intruder looked like he might explode. "I will knock your teeth into the next county."

"You're not getting any pictures. And you're not threatening us a moment more." Uncle David took a step closer, so that he was mere inches from the man. "Now, get in your car and return to the hole you came from, or the police will haul you away."

Abby knew he hadn't called the police. What was Uncle David doing?

The man took a step back.

Uncle David! She wanted to hug him. The man was afraid of her uncle!

"You'll pay for this. You'll pay for this." He almost whimpered and ran down the aisle, past the kids, letting the door slam behind him. His tires kicked gravel into the air as he raced down the road back toward Colbey.

Uncle David hurried by the table as well, and Abby pushed Josh to follow.

By the time they got close enough to hear, Uncle David was asking, "No other phone closer? The airport is the closest?"

"It's on this edge of town."

He looked frustrated, but held his tongue. When his gaze met Abby's, he gave a comforting smile. "Let's go make some phone calls. We've got work to do."

CHAPTER NINE
May, 1925 - Twenty Minutes Later
Nashville Flight Club

*J*osh couldn't stop staring at the timbers that held the massive hangar high overhead. He also couldn't take his eyes off the private planes that sat under the impressive building.

They waited by the car that was parked near a large single-engine plane in the center of the concrete pad. A mechanic worked on a bi-plane nearby, but the only other person they saw was Uncle David leaning against the wall, talking on the phone.

He hung up and walked toward them. "Miss Emma is just fine. She showed the letter to her father, but then it was stolen from his desk. I think they needed it for evidence of where the film is. We'll have to figure out how they knew about the letter later. I called the police in Colbey, and they're contacting the county sheriff to look into the matter. At least he didn't follow us here, but I wish we'd had a phone in the café to really nail that guy."

"The police will protect Miss Emma." Josh was relieved they'd finally called.

Uncle David put a hand on Josh's shoulder. "That's right." He faced the plane. "Now, we need to decide what to do."

"What do you mean?" Abby asked. "We're not going to Arizona?"

"Well, Miss Emma thinks we should go get the film." He let go of Josh's shoulder. "She feels the police have things under control in Colbey. She also said that we should beat the intruder to the film."

"I agree with Miss Emma," Josh said quickly. She was smart.

"Me too." Abby took a few steps under the plane's wing and gave the tire a soft kick. "Let's fly this thing."

"I think you're right. We should get this film. We'll have burglars every day at this point if we don't resolve this."

The airplane mechanic told them the plane was ready to go, so Uncle David helped them into the front cockpit, strapped belts over their shoulders and across their waists, then stepped off the ladder.

Several sets of goggles and blankets lay on the plane floor, and they put the glass lenses on. A quick glance in front of him told Josh that he had no instruments, no access to working the plane. Uncle David would be doing all the flying.

"Josh, this is so amazing!" Beside him, Abby grabbed his shoulder and shook until he felt his arm might fall off. "We're sitting here, out in the open. What if the plane rolls upside down and we fall out?"

"You're scared. You always get excited when you're scared." Josh thought about the mechanics of doing a barrel roll. "Gravity and inertia would keep us in the cockpit, even if we didn't have a harness on."

"Scared and excited are the same feeling," she said, sitting as high as the belt would allow and looking behind her. "You just have to choose which one you want."

Josh looked behind them. Uncle David crawled into the second cockpit. After he looked down, probably at the instrument panel, he looked up at them. He gave a thumbs up signal, one Abby returned.

There was a loud *pop*. The engine blade spun. The rumble was so loud Josh thought the vibration would shake the airplane apart.

They taxied from the hangar's shadow into the late afternoon sun, then past other large, curve-roofed hangars to a long grass strip.

Josh glanced inside the hangar. Was that a Model T pulling to the front? The intruder got out of his car. Josh motioned to Uncle David, who was looking down, and suddenly the thunder of the engines was deafening.

The plane gained speed and the engine roared even louder. They bumped along the grass for a moment, then the ride suddenly went smooth and the ground dropped away.

They rose, higher and higher, until they flew through the clouds. For about half an hour, Abby giggled, so Josh knew she was afraid, but then the excitement wore off and she fell asleep, her head on his shoulder. Josh peered through the waning daylight at tiny farmhouses and fields that looked like a long quilt.

He glanced behind, and Uncle David gave him another thumbs up.

They flew for hours, following railroad tracks.

The engine's roar quieted a bit, and Josh's heart skipped a beat. They slowly descended, and he realized they were about to land. Lower, lower, until the wheels touched an empty gravel road.

When the propeller and engine stopped, Josh still heard the roar in his ears.

Uncle David jumped out of his cockpit, using the step in the fuselage, then opened a hatch door near the front. He pulled out a can of gas.

Abby sat up, her face puffy and her hair messy. "We there?"

"Just refueling," Josh said.

She sat back and closed her eyes.

As he poured in the gas, Uncle David chatted with him. "This is a De Havilland DH-4B. Mail carrier. The boys in Nashville used the cargo hold, where the mail was stored, to haul fuel. We have enough gas on board to fly across the United States."

"When will we get there?" Josh asked.

"In the morning, probably."

"Is flying in the dark safe?"

"Compass and stars. And a flashlight." He looked up and smiled. "By morning, we'll be in Arizona. Kingman." He dropped the empty can and went to get another. "Make sure you and Abby bundle up with blankets. It'll be cold tonight."

Josh covered Abby as they rose again to cloud level. He watched the sunset, thinking how much Mom and Dad would have loved this. He woke Abby, and she glanced up, watched for a while, then as darkness covered the earth, she went back to sleep.

Josh thought about how amazing the earth was. There was only one job he would ever do, and that was study science, specifically dinosaurs. He'd not thought much about them since Mom and Dad died, but now, as the world seemed to crawl under him, he dreamed about what the dinosaurs would be doing right now if they still roamed the earth. Bedding down? Finishing their feast? Spending time with their young?

Below them, the vast black emptiness stretched on forever. Above, the stars sparkled with such brilliance and seemed so close Josh felt as if they flew among them. The last thing he saw before he fell asleep was a cloud of swirling color. He smiled. The Milky Way, like he'd never seen it before...

Jolted awake, Josh lifted his head and looked around as the biplane rolled to a stop. The engine revved, cut, and again, the silence seemed so much louder than the motor's roar. A farmhouse. Barn. A few goats. And a very, very brown desert.

The engine's metal clicked as it cooled.

The desert stretched around them, and the morning sun sent blues and reds and oranges against mesquite.

Abby lifted her head. "How long have I slept?" Her hair shot up at a funny angle on one side.

"Most of the day yesterday, and all night," Uncle David said, hopping out of the plane. He removed his leather cap and goggles, stripped off his gloves, rubbed his face. "Don't you remember stopping and using the restroom in Oklahoma?"

"Oh yeah."

Uncle David helped them out, then told them to wait by the plane. He started for the nearby farmhouse.

He returned a few minutes later with the farmer's town car, five dollars poorer for renting it. They all loaded in, and after Uncle David got his bearings on the map, they started down the road and took a right past a sign that said Kingman. He took a bite of hardboiled egg from the food Miss Emma had prepared for them. "We need to go to town to get supplies for a trek in the desert, then we'll drive to the canyon and start our hike."

Josh ran his finger along the map. "Did we really fly over the Grand Canyon last night?"

"We did. We're on the south side now." Uncle David wiped his brow as the broiling wind whipped through the car. "Boy, it's hot here."

"We know." Josh sighed. "We've been here before."

The heat wasn't the only thing that bothered him. This was the location of their last adventure with Mom and Dad. The pain grew stronger the closer they came to the hotel where the police officer had told him and Abby that their parents had just died.

The main street traffic consisted of a few horses and carriages plus several cars. On either side of the street, businesses with large signs blocked the view of distant mountains he remembered. People strolled along the sidewalks.

So peaceful.

A car buzzed past them.

Josh nudged Abby. "Did you see what I just saw?"

Through the back window, he saw two men wearing pin-striped suits. But that wasn't what scared him.

He spied the barrel of a tommy gun.

Josh groaned. This was going to be harder than he'd first thought. Not just hard. Deadly.

Uncle David slowed the car and turned into a mechanic's shop. "This'll just take a second." He closed the door behind him.

"I'm going with him." Abby tugged on the handle. "You coming, Josh?"

"Abby," he said, motioning back to the main road. "I just saw a car full of mobsters. Right here in town. You'd better stay with me."

"I gotta go to the bathroom. Uncle David will keep me

safe." She hopped out of the car and hurried to his side.

Josh waited for a few moments, watching for mobsters, and then noticed an article in a newspaper on the floor. He picked it up and started reading. About a monster. In the Grand Canyon, the Mogollon Monster roamed, an animal with white hair and white beard that fell to its knees. The beast had been sighted again in an outlying canyon.

"Probably a grizzly bear," he said to himself.

But mobsters and monsters? Could their journey be any more harrowing?

CHAPTER TEN

May, 1925 - Fifteen Minutes Later
Kingman, Arizona

Josh jumped as Abby threw open the door.

He'd been so focused on the article, he didn't notice she was approaching.

"Josh, you've got to hear what Uncle David just did."

"You scared me."

"Listen to me. Before he gets here. He didn't know I was there. He paid a mechanic to look at the wreckage of Mom and Dad's car. It's still at the police station. And Uncle David told him to look for foul play. Gave the mechanic ten bucks, then told him to call the house with what he finds."

Josh set down the paper. "Uncle David did that?"

She nodded, then spotted him coming out of the garage. "He doesn't know I know. I'd been in the bathroom, then overheard him.

Uncle David walked toward them, then paused in front of the car and said, "Let's get something to eat. Grab the map."

Finally, time to plan.

They crossed the street to a café with a huge sign that offered meatloaf for a dime. They entered to see only a few other customers. Their food came quickly, and they ate while studying the map.

Josh pointed to the map's edge. "Here's where the road ends and the trail starts. A man who lives at the top of the trail has mules people can rent to take down into the canyon. It's about a six-mile hike."

"Six miles." Uncle David nodded.

Josh glanced at his sister. "Do you think you can climb the falls, Abby?"

Abby clapped her hands. "Easy peasy!"

Josh grinned. Finally. They could get the proof they needed. But the thought niggling at the back of Josh's brain finally crystallized.

The mobsters had been driving out of town, headed along the road that would take them to the canyon. Had the intruder been following them to confirm they were on their way to Arizona, to confirm the film was inside the Havasupai Reserve? There was a lot of territory to cover, and the canister was small. They would never find it. Would they even try? They certainly weren't dressed for the desert. Either way, he'd better tell his uncle about the mobsters in Arizona.

"Uncle David? There's something I need to tell you."

Following Uncle David, they strolled into a clothing store located inside the Brunswick Hotel. The smell of fresh clothes and leather washed over Josh. A woman with strong perfume stepped up to help Uncle David trade his slacks, jacket, and tie for a pair of thick, wool-twill pants. They were too long, but the woman hemmed and pressed them while he tried on shirts. He chose a thin, brown shirt but ignored the leather jacket the clerk—her husband—suggested.

She looked up from her machine. "The coat's discounted. Ten dollars."

Uncle David held up the jacket. "Not much of a discount."

"That's because it comes with this." The seamstress's husband, standing behind the wood counter, held up a large leather satchel that had a flap over the top.

Uncle David opened the bag.

Abby sucked in a breath. "It's beautiful."

Uncle David shook his head. "These satchels aren't normally made for fieldwork. Although…I haven't seen one so…" He glanced at Josh and Abby. "So perfect."

Abby nodded. "I love it."

He slung the strap over his head.

Josh had to admit, the satchel *was* perfect.

"Why are you discounting the jacket and the satchel, too?"

"This is Arizona." The man motioned outside. "It's spring now. Why would anyone need a jacket?"

Uncle David stepped into the dressing room and came out in his new shirt and pants. He laced his new boots and tossed the jacket to Josh. He reached for a trilby hat hanging on a nearby rack, then paused.

Josh knew what his uncle was thinking and spoke his thoughts for him. "The hat's brim is too narrow. The desert is hot."

"Right." He picked up a fedora and set it carefully on his head.

Abby adjusted the brim. "Women wear fedoras."

"And men." Uncle David glanced in the mirror. "When working in the field, you use the best equipment possible, no matter the fashion."

He threw the satchel strap around his neck. "How do I look?"

Abby clapped. "Like an adventurer!"

Even Josh had to admit his uncle was a dashing figure. "Like Dad."

Uncle David squeezed Josh's shoulder. "Let's go get that film."

The couple in the shop let them change from their travel clothes into safari gear. Now Josh felt ready for an adventure.

Uncle David parked the car behind a giant rock, hidden from the dirt road and the trail leading into the canyon.

Loaded with food and canteens in their backpacks, they rounded the boulder.

They started north, and Josh judged from the sun that it was about nine o'clock. They came upon a small shack beside an empty corral.

"We hired mules from here once," Josh said.

Uncle David knocked and a bewhiskered man opened the warped, wooden door, and the rusted hinges creaked.

"What kin I do ya fer?" the man asked as Uncle David approached.

"Horses. Need to rent some."

"Mules is what we got," the man said. "But right now, mules is what we ain't got. All rented out."

Josh noticed Abby step away, going in search of mules, he guessed. He took a few steps back so he could listen and still see Abby.

Uncle David lifted his wallet. "Not for any price?"

The man scrunched his weathered face and squinted at his uncle. "How much? Not that I have any animals, but how much?"

"Twenty-five?"

"Nope." The man snorted., "Ain't got any. And wouldn't rent 'em for such a measly amount."

Josh thought Uncle David's offer was plenty high, but he kept his mouth shut. Out of the corner of his eye, he saw Abby cross the trailhead and slip behind a tall boulder.

Oh, you're kidding.

"Path's closed today," the man said. "Closed, on account of…" He rubbed his head, looked at the sky, squinted again. "Military maneuvers. The government took all my mules."

Josh started toward Abby.

"Uncle David, Uncle David!" Abby called from behind the hill. "There're mules over here!"

The man had lied. Josh glanced up to see Uncle David's reaction.

Uncle David set his hands on his hips and gave the wizened man a look. "Must have been in a prairie dog hole?"

"They told me." The man scratched the side of his head. "Told me to say I didn't have any more, so I done hid 'em. Government, you know. Military maneuvers, guns." He looked away. "I kin rent 'em to ya fer seventy-five."

Josh frowned. That was near robbery!

Uncle David talked the price down.

Fifteen minutes later, they were descending into the canyon on the backs of surefooted but cautious mules, saddles squeaking, Uncle David leading the way.

"Uncle David," Josh called from his position behind Abby and her mule. "You don't really believe what he said about the military, do you?"

He turned, his wide-brimmed hat shadowing his face. "If we come across the soldiers, we'll just say I'm a professor teaching students." He smiled and repeated Abby's "Easy peasy."

Josh groaned.

Uncle David laughed. "Just think of it this way. The soldiers will keep us safe."

For a brilliant professor, his uncle seemed awfully naive at times.

Abby turned around and whispered, "Is he putting us on?"

Uncle David tugged on the reigns, stopped, and looked at them. "No, no I don't believe him. I was hoping to keep you from worrying. But you're too smart for that, aren't you?"

"Yeah," Josh said.

They kept riding.

The only sound was the gravel crunching beneath the mule's hooves as they slowly navigated past huge boulders, scrub, mesquite trees, yucca plants, and spiny cactus. Now that they were back in the desert, the encyclopedias in his

mind were busy flipping pages, giving names to all the plants. A flowering fernbush. Banana yucca. Agave. Brittle brush. Western honey mesquite.

His mule smelled like sweat.

Josh had ridden this trail twice—once down with his parents, then up when running from the mobsters. Now, traveling the path a third time, memories of his parents bubbled to the surface. Abby must have been remembering too, because her head was bowed and he heard her crying quietly.

"This is how we find justice," Josh said quietly. "For Mom and Dad, I mean. We take little steps to find who did it."

Abby set her pith helmet on the saddle horn, covered her face with her hands and began to sob.

Uncle David slipped off his mule and rushed to her side. As he pulled Abby into his arms, Josh dropped from his saddle too.

"We miss them," Josh managed, the pain welling in his throat.

Uncle David opened his arm. Josh took off his wide-brimmed hat and leaned against his uncle's strong shoulder.

"I miss them too." Uncle David's deep voice vibrated through Josh. "I shouldn't have brought you two out here."

"Doesn't work that way." Josh took a breath to clear some of the pain. "You go to the places and work through the feelings.

"We have to visit where we last saw our parents." Abby choked, then continued. "Crying helps."

Josh leaned against his uncle, and for the first time, he felt like the tears might be helping him heal.

But within ten minutes, they were back on the trail, joking and laughing. Josh felt better than he had in a long time. To pass the time, Abby made monkey sounds and Josh guessed which monkey species. Her interpretations were spot on, as were his guesses.

"You know all this from your trip to Brazil?" Uncle David asked.

"Yep!" Then Abby made the sound of a parrot.

Josh's mule lumbered on, footstep after footstep, down into the canyon until they arrived at the level valley. They followed the gravel path for miles without encountering another soul, not even a javelina, coyote, or rattlesnake. Not even the indigenous people who lived in this area seemed to be around.

A hot breeze blew dust into his face. He wiped away the sweat and grime with his long sleeve and thought about rolling up the cuffs. But he knew from experience the cloth protected his skin from the sun.

The trail followed a dry stream bed, but soon, from one side of the canyon wall, water trickled along the desert sand, and the path followed the stream.

"We're getting close," Josh called. "In just a minute, we'll need to take the trail off to the right."

When the fork in the trail appeared, Uncle David stopped. Abby's mule came to a gradual halt, but Josh's animal almost hit Abby's before waking enough to stop.

"This is way to the falls?" Uncle David pointed toward the left.

"Yes, but to the right is the cliffs where Mom and Dad were documenting pictographs." Josh motioned toward the opposite path. "It's beautiful this direction. Wish we had time to see it."

Uncle David removed his hat and looked at the sky. "We're going to need to move a bit faster. It's almost one o'clock, and we've still got to find Havasupai Falls, then ride all the way back. It'll be nearing sunset by the time we get back, and that's if we hurry."

Josh pulled out his canteen and twisted off the lid. He took a drink. "Okay, let's go."

He screwed the lid back on the canteen and stowed it in his pack. He waved a hand.

They rode past gambel oaks, sage, and wildflowers watered by Havasu Creek. The scent of sage hung in the air.

"Uncle David," Josh said. "The stream? It has calcium carbonate. That's $CaCO_3$. Did you know the water changes paths every year? New rocks are made from the limestone! That's why it looks so clear and blue-green. It's because of the chemicals."

He'd spent hours imagining dinosaurs wandering through the canyon, the flora and fauna from a distant past. He sighed. Oh, to have lived in those days. He wished it was *his* footprints beside that dinosaur's tracks.

The smell of warm juniper and the roar of the falls brought him back to the present.

"Look up there." Uncle David pointed.

In the distance, leaning against a rock, two black dots grew larger and came into focus. The two men stood, one dressed in a brown suit, the other in black. Each held a tommy gun.

Beyond the men, about a football field away, was Havasupai Falls, the one he and Abby had jumped. That day seemed like a lifetime ago. The canyon here was tight, closed in. They wouldn't be able to go around these guys.

Uncle David glanced back at them.

Abby frowned. "Can they see us? Think they'll shoot us?"

Josh didn't say anything. Would the mobsters hurt them now that there would be no witnesses? Why was Uncle David pressing on? This was dangerous. In the extreme.

A few minutes later, the two men stepped into their path. They didn't point their guns, but each kept a hand on his weapon.

Uncle David stopped. "Wait here. I'm going to talk to them." His voice was deeper than Josh had ever heard, and he had the firm, in-command look he'd had when confronting the intruder. Uncle David clicked his tongue, and his mule started forward.

One man held up a hand as he approached.

"Josh, they're two of the ones who destroyed the evidence, remember? The short one with the crowbar, and the fat one with the pickax?"

"Yeah, I remember." He pictured them in his head. "We're missing the tall, skinny one."

After a minute of discussion that Josh couldn't quite make out, Abby hopped off her mule.

"Josh, I've got to go to the bathroom," she said, sliding off the mule. "Distract them."

"*What?*"

"I gotta go."

"Abby, this is really a bad time."

"They're not going to let us in. See, that one keeps shaking his head. Distract them."

"Abby—"

"First I'll ask Uncle David. Then, while I'm off in the bushes, I'll really be climbing the cliff."

"This is the worst idea I ever—"

She ran toward Uncle David and the mobsters.

"Abby...you've got to be kidding me." He sighed and dismounted to follow her.

When he got closer, he could hear his uncle's stern voice. "We came to see the falls."

One of the men grabbed the cactus spine he'd been chewing from his mouth. "Sorry, mister." He flung the sharp barb to the side. "Like I says, falls is closed."

"Yeah," the other man said. "By order of the...of the federal government. It's some..." The man glanced at his partner. "Some military thing."

"That's right." The other one sneezed. "Military."

"Look, we've driven a long way to see the falls. Wouldn't take more than say, twenty minutes. Then we'll leave."

Hired men. Only told what they needed to know. Josh realized they might not know to be looking out for a man and two children.

Abby stopped near her uncle's side.

The other man straightened. "Mister. I don't know how many times we gots to tell you, but the canyon is closed. You ain't even supposed to be down here. You was supposed to be stopped up at the entrance. Now go."

"Closed for how long?"

"Weeks."

"Months."

"Maybe a year."

The men glanced at Abby, then at Josh, who stopped behind his sister. Josh studied their faces. No sigh of recognition. But Josh was pretty sure these were the men who'd helped destroy the evidence.

"Can we look at the falls now? I want to go swimming." Abby used her whiney voice.

Josh normally hated the sound, but he had to hold back a smile as a rush of pride swelled in his chest. She was a good actor.

"No, the military is working in the area. Going there would be unsafe." Uncle David rubbed his neck.

Abby pouted. "I gotta go. To the bathroom."

Uncle David glanced at the men, then back at her. "This is a really bad time. You'll just have to hold it until we're near the falls and can find thicker bushes to hide in."

"But I gotta go *now*," she whined, her voice shrill. Abby crossed her legs and did a little dance. "P-l-e-ease."

One of the men waved his gun. "All right, go over there behind those rocks. But don't dawdle."

She was already running toward the falls. Josh could hear the water's roar.

"Not that way!" one man said.

The other man asked, "You want I should go get her?"

"Nah, leave her be. Just keep an eye on her whereabouts."

"Hey," Josh said. "Watch? You're not going to watch my sister go to the bathroom, are you?" He had to distract them. "Can I look at your gun?" Josh reached for one of the men's weapons.

He jerked his gun away. "Get back, kid. Hands off. You trying to get yourself killed?"

"Thompson submachine gun." Josh looked at Uncle David. *Please, help me here.* "Not cheap. Probably cost half as much a Model T. Those two guns together could be traded for a car."

"Marines, boy. We were Marines. Military, remember?"

"I heard the postal service bought some guns due to so many robberies lately."

"Yeah, something like that."

"If you're military, why aren't you in uniform?"

One man looked at the other. "Military secret. Can't tell you."

"Were you in the Great War?"

"Don't want to talk about it, kid."

"Josh…" Uncle David chided him in a low voice. Josh wasn't sure if he'd caught on yet, but maybe talking about the war was taking things too far.

He saw movement on the cliff wall, then beneath the falls. A figure disappeared behind the water and emerged on the other side.

His sister had made it to the waterfall!

"Hey! Where is that girl?" One of the men started to turn around.

Josh had to think fast. He gasped. "Look!"

Uncle David twirled. "What? What is it Josh?"

Josh ran toward a flower he recognized. He dropped to his knees. "Look, Uncle David!"

His uncle hurried over, the two men right behind him.

They peered down. One of the mobsters growled, "What is it?"

The encyclopedia opened in Josh's mind. "Epipactis gigantea." He held both hands around the plant, as if framing a sacred object.

The men stared at the flower. "Epi…what?"

Josh clasped his head with both hands. "My goodness, this is swell beyond words. Epipactis gigantea!" He looked up to see blank looks on the men's faces. "Giant helleborine?"

The men shook their heads.

"This is the rarest orchid known to man!"

The beautiful plant with red, brown, and yellow petals blossoming on the desert floor was, indeed, an Epipactis gigantea. However, it was the most common orchid on the planet.

"This is a great find, Josh," Uncle David said.

But he was trying too hard. He was a biologist, after all, and knew plants intimately.

"See how the flower looks as if it is about to eat someone. It has a mouth below, and eyes up here."

The men leaned down. "This flower don't look mean," one said. Then, he turned to the other one. "Think we can sell it?"

Josh chanced a look at Abby and saw her scramble back behind the waterfall again, one handhold at a time.

"I'll let you have the orchid, gentlemen." Uncle David stood. "But don't pick it, or it'll die. Maybe you could sell tickets for people to come and see it."

While the men discussed what they should do with the orchid, Abby appeared from out of the bushes. Her ponytail was undone and her hair was plastered across her forehead from water. Drops flew from her clothes as she walked.

If the bad guys noticed she was wet, they didn't say anything.

Uncle David motioned with his head. "No need to keep these gentlemen from their duties. How long did you say the canyon is closed?"

"Weeks," one said.

"Months," said the other.

Uncle David sighed. "Well, we might as well get on with our vacation. Maybe another time, kids." He tipped his hat then motioned to the mules. "Good day, gents."

They climbed into their saddles, and Uncle David turned

his mule around and started back up the trail. Abby followed, and Josh tapped his mule's sides to trail them.

Across the hot canyon floor they rode until they turned around a rock wall, hidden from the men's sight.

Abby cleared her throat. "I couldn't find the canister." She sounded as if she was about to cry. "I couldn't see from below the ledge. I need to get on top of the waterfall and work my way down!"

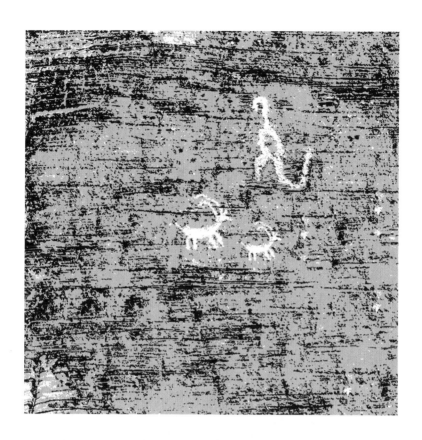

CHAPTER ELEVEN

May, 1925 - Five Minutes Later
Havasupai Canyon, Arizona

Josh checked behind them for the two men guarding the falls. "What are we going to do now?"

"Why were they guarding the falls?" Uncle David asked, ignoring his question, probably to give himself time to think.

"Because our camp was farther down, and they were searching the area?" It was the only idea Josh could come up with. "What are we going to do?" he said again.

"We need to find a way to the top of those falls, but these

cliffs are too steep, too tall." Uncle David took a drink from his canteen.

"I have an idea." Abby took off her pith helmet and worked on her pigtails. "Remember the scaffolding? We could climb up from there! I bet it's still up."

"That's right!" Josh knew the right answer when he heard it. "We just need to take the route back to the dig."

"Let's go look," Uncle David said.

They guided their mules the other direction at the fork in the road.

Other than their lingering dust, the trail was empty.

The new path was less traveled, and their mules had to pick their way past rocks and trees. Heat pressed on Josh's back, and he wished for just a few moments' break, just a dip in the creek. But now that they'd veered away from the river, the air seemed hotter, more oppressive. Sweat poured down his face, which sucked away the energy from his muscles.

He removed his hat and wiped his brow. Abby took off her pith helmet and did the same.

When they finally reached the end of the canyon, they saw the scaffolding—nearly eight stories tall—working its way up the side of the wall, just like Josh remembered.

Josh brought his mule to a halt and listened. He thought he heard voices.

Uncle David held up a hand and he and Abby stopped too. Yes, someone was coming from behind.

Uncle David pointed to a clump of rocks. "Quick," he whispered. "Behind those rocks."

They dismounted and tugged their mules behind the outcropping. They peered over the edge. Josh gripped the rock in front of him.

Sixteen legs—twelve with hooves and six with boots—had left too much dust floating in the air.

A man was talking as he stepped into view. "But we found out about the man and kids too late to know who we was looking for. They said it were the same kids we chased earlier."

"Doesn't matter now."

The two men who'd guarded the falls ambled along. Their guns hung loosely in hand.

"What do you mean 'doesn't matter'?"

The men were coming closer. Abby and Uncle David rubbed their mules' noses to keep them quiet. Josh did the same.

"The entrance by the mule keeper was unguarded. But I bet it's guarded now. And we're going to sweep the canyon before dark. We'll find that film the boss is looking for. And those kids."

"We just gotta make sure they're not down this canyon path?"

"Yeah."

Josh held his breath as the men neared. Dust still hung in the air! The men would notice.

"This is not what we was paid for. I mean look at my shoes! They're ruined."

"That's 'cause you're used to the city."

The two men, who lived in the city, didn't know the meaning of a cloud of dust hovering around a perfect place to hide.

Josh held his breath.

Surely, they could see the hoof prints that led to their hiding place.

"I'm hot. And they're not here. Let's keep moving." The

man's fine black suit must be brutal in this sun.

The other one took off his jacket and slung it over his shoulder. "Fire a few rounds." The other man held up his tommy gun. "That'll scare 'em if they're here."

Machine gun fire from so close would scare the mules, and then they'd be discovered for sure. Josh put his arm around his mule's neck and held his hands over the beast's ears, but he had a feeling it wouldn't help. He scrunched close to the mule's side, ready for the loud burst.

"Don't fire," the other gangster said. "The others will think we found the kids. Look, there's the end of the canyon, anyway. Let's go back."

The two men retreated the way they'd come.

Josh released the breath he'd been holding. "How did they know to look for us?" he whispered.

Uncle David looked at the sun. "Someone searching the camp may know more about what's going on than these two. We've got to hurry, or it will be after dark before we get back to the plane."

"But you heard them," Abby said in a high-pitched voice. "The entrance is cut off!"

Her uncle grabbed her arms. "Abby. Abby look at me." His voice was soft. "We'll be okay. One problem at a time. Let's go get that film."

"Okay," she whispered. "I'll be okay. We have to find the film."

He turned away. "Let's go." And tugged on the reins.

"Okay," she said again. "I'll be okay. I'll be okay."

No. Abby wasn't okay. Her hands shook. "Uncle David," Josh said. "Wait a second."

Abby repeated, "I'll be okay."

His uncle turned. "What now? We have to—"

"She's gone through too much," Josh said. "It adds up for her. Getting past those two monsters earlier, and now this close call. It's too much" Josh snapped his fingers to get her attention. "Abby, see that tree? Go run around it." He took her mule's reins. "At the ready? Are you set? Go!"

She hopped from the mule and dashed off, kicking up dust behind her.

"She has so much energy when she's scared," Josh told Uncle David, as his sister disappeared around the tree. "Sometimes she needs to move to calm down. I remember once..."

His voice trailed off. Abby didn't return from behind the low bushes.

Josh frowned.

"Maybe she's taking another bathroom break," Uncle David suggested.

"Josh! Uncle David! Come here!" Abby sounded excited. "You've got to see this."

"She always does this," Josh muttered. "We'd better go see. She won't let up until we do."

They marched toward her hiding spot and both stopped.

Uncle David stood, unmoving. He just stared.

About eye level, red pictographs on the cliff wall depicted prehistoric animals.

"Oh, my... That's an ibex." Uncle David's voice sounded quiet and far away. He stared at the paintings, his mouth open.

Josh grunted. "We've got to get to the scaffolding, but yes, that's an ibex. I've seen more around here. I took pictures of them."

"But how would they have known..."

"Dad never found ibex bones," Abby said, using her scientist voice, something Josh hadn't heard since Mom and Dad died. "There's no way prehistoric peoples should have known ibex exist."

"We've got to go." Josh pulled on his mule's reins.

Uncle David worked his way through the brush and touched the wall. "Red sandstone. The artists stood here, looks like they used their right hands," he said, pointing at the paintings. "Iron in the sandstone provides the red color. Here's another ibex. Wait. Here's another. A...a dinosaur! That's... And an elephant. No, this is impossible."

He opened his satchel. "I need to get some rubbings. I wish I'd brought a camera."

"That's how we ran into trouble the first time," Josh muttered. "I'm going on."

"I'll go with you," Abby said.

Leaving their uncle behind, Josh hiked up the tiny ravine. Abby followed.

To his relief, the scaffolding still leaned firm against the cliff wall. "Thank you, Dr. Hubbard, for not taking this down."

Metal poles were connected by smaller, interlaced cables. Boards stretched between the poles, making platforms up the cliff's side.

Josh tied the mules to a mesquite tree.

"Let's go." Abby said, just as Uncle David walked up. She headed straight for the ladder. "We'll get to the rim in no time, and I'll find that film."

Josh climbed up first, and the three scaled the metal rungs up the side of the scaffolding, past the first four platforms. Josh paused, already out of breath. Four more levels to the top. Memories flooded in, unbidden. He remembered when his father had shown him the paintings along this level, the ibex painted halfway up the face. Dad had explained the unlikelihood of the African animal being seen in Arizona. No ibex fossils were ever found, so how could a North American native know what an African ibex looked like?

Josh hadn't discovered the dinosaur and human tracks until the final day—the last time their family had been together.

The scaffolding didn't reach the top of the cliff. They'd have to climb the rest of the way. By rope.

Uncle David crawled onto the highest level and glanced down at them, his eyes large. "This is high." He spread his feet wide and pulled a long stretch of rope from his satchel. With a quick movement, he tied one end into a lasso.

Josh raised his eyebrows. Perhaps Uncle David was better at outdoor stuff than he thought.

As Abby climbed onto the top plank of the scaffolding, Uncle David muttered, "I've never done this before."

Twirling the rope like a cowboy, he flung the loop high above them. It caught a large boulder. "Well, what do you know? Not bad. Now, let's hope I don't pull the rock down on us."

He gave the rope a strong tug, then yanked at it with all his weight. It held. He smiled. "I'll go up first, then you come up, and I'll help you over the top."

Searching out footholds, he pulled himself up the side of the canyon. At the top, he managed to get his legs onto the ledge, crawled over and disappeared. A second later, he leaned into view. "Josh, your turn."

Josh gripped the rope with both hands and started up. Uncle David had made the climb look easy, but a few feet off

the ground, Josh slipped and rubbed his hands raw on the rope. He crashed back to the platform, causing the scaffolding to shudder.

"Here, Josh, like this." Abby grabbed the rope and marched up the side of the cliff, her arms grasping one handhold over the next, as if floating, until she scrambled over the edge. Her climb looked even easier than Uncle David's had.

Josh looked below at the empty valley. The mobsters could be coming any minute. He took a deep breath, gripped the rope, and started up the side of the cliff, using his feet to push upward and his arms to pull his body toward the top. He took a step, and then another before he slipped down again.

He paused, exhausted. This wasn't working. He shook his head and slid back to the plank, gasping for breath. "I can't make it."

"Sure you can." Abby called from above. "Just keep pulling yourself up."

He looked at his burned hands. "You go ahead. I'll get a head start back to the car." He would avoid the mobsters as best he could.

He tried to move his fingers and winced.

Uncle David looked over the edge and Abby glanced from him to Josh. "He wants to go back to the car."

"Josh." Uncle David shook his head. "That's a terrible idea. Just wait for us at the main trail."

Relieved, Josh lifted a sore arm to wave goodbye, then rubbed his hands on his pants. "If I get in trouble, I'll meet you back at the car."

They disappeared. Josh turned and looked across the canyon. So quiet out here. He was alone. All alone, in a hot, narrow canyon where men with tommy guns were searching for him.

And rattlesnakes.

As he climbed down the scaffolding ladder, he vowed that when they returned to Colbey, he would start climbing and running—anything to get into better shape.

His father had always told him to stay active. *You can't have incredible adventures unless you're able to keep up with others.* Dad had made him exercise. However, without his father around, he'd done nothing but lie on his bed reading books.

Josh wandered a quarter mile back the way they'd come, tugging the mules along, three sets of reins in one hand.

He passed a wide spot along the creek where his family had pitched camp before finding their permanent camp several months ago. Before grief could overcome him again, he focused on watching out for the mobster guards. If he got too lonely, he could yell really loud and the guards would surely come running.

Nope. He wasn't that lonely.

He arrived where the trail split, and he pulled the mules off the path and settled them behind a boulder, then sat on a rock to keep watch.

Heat reflected off the sand and gravel as the sun beat down from above. He searched the ground for snakes, scorpions, and other potential hazards, but his mind soon wandered.

What if he were a dinosaur, the Coelophysis that had made the tracks he'd discovered before the men destroyed them with crowbars? Oh, what he wouldn't give to see one of those dinosaurs walking toward him through the canyon.

But when they'd inhabited the earth, the landscape wouldn't have been so dry. The canyon walls shimmered and faded in front of him. He could smell the rainforest and hear the jungle animals. An ibex galloped along, a Coelophysis close on its hooves, kicking up dust.

He imagined other animals thundering by and turned to watch the images his mind had conjured so well.

The picture shimmered again, but instead of a lineup of wild beasts, he saw four armed men, tommy guns at their side. Their black suits and hats looked out of place in the wild, remote desert landscape.

He recognized them. The two, guarding the falls, a short man and the fat man, were on the left. The tall, skinny man had broken the tracks was there, too, and a strong man he never saw before marched on the right.

A flock of birds shot by Josh. Two mule deer bounded up the canyon, spotted him, and dove off to the side. A loud thrashing sound echoed against the walls, and he jumped behind a saguaro cactus, its arms extending high, like a giant.

Then, into view, strode men in newsboy caps, fedoras, and straw hats, toward him.

He counted. Besides the four men in suits, there were six others walked in the long row, sticks in one hand, and pistols in the other. The six wore long-sleeved button up shirts, better suited for this weather, with rough chaps over their Levi's. All six men were weathered, as if they were locals who understood the desert.

A boom shook the chasm, and it took a moment for Josh to realize the sound was a gunshot. The blast echoed through the canyon.

The thin mobster with a tommy gun marched toward one

end of the line. "Find something?"

"Rattler. He won't bother us no more."

The skinny mobster set his machine gun on his hip. "Call out when you find those kids. They'll know where the film is."

"Right, boss."

Something rustled behind him, and Josh turned to look. To his horror, the mules had escaped and were racing right toward the men!

"Hey, look what we got here. Looks like they're close by. Let's go."

The men were coming right at him! And they were spread across the entire canyon! Without a doubt, they would find him.

How far up the trail was the car? Two miles? Three? More like five.

Should he hide, let the men pass by, then run to Uncle David and Abby to warn them? No, the mobsters were combing every inch of sand. They would find him no matter where he hid.

They'd shot at him and Abby before, but surely, they wouldn't go as far as to kill them.

They killed your parents.

Panic gave his limbs life.

Josh turned and sprinted up the trail away from the men. *Please let me be out of view.* He didn't bother turning around.

He avoided the open path, hugging the wall, swerving around boulders and bushes in hopes he wouldn't be seen. Not until he'd passed a long outcropping and was completely out of breath did he slow and return to the trail. But he kept up a jog.

Why did he always have to run?

Was it five hundred miles?

Five bazillion miles later, he recognized the terrain. He was getting closer to the car.

His muscles felt like butter in a hot pan. He stopped to rub his legs. Sweat dripped from his face into the dust at his feet.

Oh, how he hoped Abby had already found the film! *God, please*, he prayed. But the mobsters stood between his sister and his uncle and freedom!

How long did it take for him to catch his breath? Five minutes? An hour? He glanced toward the sun, which sent spikes of light at his eyes. The sun had moved about six degrees since he'd paused to rest, which, as he looked through the encyclopedia in his mind, was just over thirty minutes. Fifteen-degree movement per hour was usual, depending on how high the sun was when corresponding to where he stood on the earth.

He grunted. He was tired. He took the last sip of water from his canteen. The rest of their supplies were on a mule, miles away by now.

Voices from behind jerked him back into the real world.

The mobsters marched into view.

His legs tingled with exhaustion, but he darted into a thicket and past a cluster of bushes. He crouched, blocking himself from view. Rocks dug into his palms as he crawled over a rise and looked down. He could see the car where they'd left it, parked behind a wall of red rocks. From his vantage point, he could also see the men getting closer and closer.

They neared enough he could've dropped a rock on them.

A man stopped, then called out. "Hey, there's a car over

here!"

The mobsters hurried to the car. "This has got to be theirs."

The other men congregated around the vehicle.

"They'll be coming back here," the thin mobster called the boss said, pointing to the car door. "Half of you march down the ravine over there and search for them."

The local men grumbled. "We weren't paid to walk this far. And it's getting late."

The boss set the tommy gun's butt on his hip. "My benefactor's got deep pockets. You'll be rewarded. Be sure to spread out again. There, make a line. They'll be hot and thirsty without water. So, they'll have to come back here. When you find the kids, bring them to me. No one else is in the canyon, so if you have to use force, I won't say anything."

Josh's heart pounded even harder. He had to do something to keep them from setting a trap for Abby and Uncle David. Start a fire? But he had no matches.

The side ravine. Across the way. What could he do to get *all* the men down the ravine?

Despite the fear that made him want to run all the way to town, he searched his brain. He had to come up with a plan, fast. *God, please help!*

In the distance, he saw two figures climbing up the trail toward him. A chill snaked up his spine.

Abby and Uncle David. With the mobsters between him and them.

Act, now, Josh. Act now.

CHAPTER TWELVE
May, 1925
Havasupai Trailhead

God, please help me, Josh prayed again.

His mind cleared.

A strange image appeared in his imagination, a beast with white hair and a beard that ended at its knees. The beast in the article he'd read earlier—the Mogollon Monster. It was a beast that was said to have roamed the Grand Canyon and outlying areas, like Havasupai.

The article said grown men who explored the canyons were afraid to be alone because of the white-haired beast.

Six men were local and knew the legend of the Mogollon Monster.

He said another quick prayer, screwed up his courage, and jumped off the rock. He ran straight for the men, arms flailing.

"Help!" he screamed. He didn't have to fake his panicked voice, wide eyes, or wild, frenzied appearance. He'd never been so frightened in his life. "Please help me! It's coming!"

The men whipped around, aiming their guns at him. He charged directly at the men in suits. "It's coming, it's coming." He leapt at the strongest man and jumped into his arms, pointing to the ravine across the way.

The man stumbled backward but kept his balance.

Hopefully Uncle David would see what was happening from the trail below.

The boss grabbed Josh by the back of his neck and wrenched him from the strong man.

"Now, what are you about?"

Josh fell to the ground.

"A monster! A beast so wretched…worse than a grizzly bear. It had to be nine feet tall! White hair. Claws this big." Josh held out his hands and curled his fingers. "It's running up that canyon!" He pointed to a ravine. "Coming straight for us!"

"You saw it, boy?" the fat mobster said. "I read about that. In the paper."

The boss dusted dirt from the muzzle of his tommy gun and pointed it at Josh. "What, Slim? You believe this kid? There's no monster."

The strong man leaned in close and said with a strong accent, "Told you we don't need these locals. This here is one of the three we're looking for."

"Listen you, there's a monster," the local man said. The others crowded around Josh. "I seen it. Camping one night. The Mogollon Monster."

"Argh!" Josh dug his fingers into his hair. "Did it have big red eyes? Did it screech like a howler monkey?"

The man's eyes widened and he stepped closer to Josh. "Yeah, yeah, that's it."

"Stop." The boss pointed his tommy gun at the men. "The boy didn't see a monster. We need to find the other two."

The local man's face turned grim. "If he's the one you told us to look for, then he don't know nothin' about the monster. Ain't he from another state?"

"Yep. Must have seen it for sure," another said.

They all started talking amongst themselves. Josh used the distraction to glance behind him. No trace of Uncle David or Abby. They must have seen and hid. He said, "Someone stop that monster. Or he will kill us all!"

"Go!" The boss waved his gun at the sky. "Go shoot the monster and be heroes. But look for the girl and man while you search the ravine. And shoot anything that moves."

Looking from side to side, the men fell into line and started cautiously toward the ravine, away from the trail.

"Slim, go with them. Make sure they stay focused."

"Got it, boss," the round man said.

As they left, the boss cupped his hands as he lit a cigarette, even though there was no wind to blow out the match. The smell of tobacco tickled his nose.

"All right, kid," he said. "You've got some explaining to do."

The strong man chuckled and stepped toward him.

Josh's heart sank. He'd whittled the large group down to three men, but it was the three most dangerous who'd stayed behind.

He hoped Uncle David and Abby were close by, because he was fresh out of ideas.

CHAPTER THIRTEEN
May, 1925 - Five Hurried Footsteps Later
Havasupai Trailhead

Running across the canyon floor, up the trail, Abby's breath came in great gasps. Without losing stride, she and Uncle David leapt over a Gila monster that chose that moment to cross their path.

"Josh would tell us all about how the Gila monster's saliva is poisonous," she puffed, "and when their teeth puncture skin, the saliva is injected."

"That I believe." Uncle David slowed as they neared a small stand of trees. "Stop. Look." He pointed. "Look at all those men leaving. But wait… There're three more mobsters between us and the car. And look! There's Josh!"

"I see him! Why are all those men leaving?"

"I don't have a clue. Maybe something Josh said?"

Her uncle's breathing reminded her of a steam engine.

She was winded, but not breathing as heavy as her uncle. "You're not used to this, are you?"

"No, not at all." He shook his head. "My classes don't usually involve running."

"We've got to get Josh."

"We'll get him. Then we've got to get the car and get out of here."

Abby looked closer. "Those men with tommy guns look mean." She glanced up at the canyon walls. "Applesauce, Josh." She closed her eyes, then looked at her uncle. "We need a distraction. A big one, to make the mobsters run."

And then the idea popped into her brain. "Uncle David, I'll start the car and rev the engine, and they'll come running. Then you hit them."

"Hit them?" He picked up a thick branch. "It's a little crazy…" He offered her a slow smile. "And you're safer in the car than anywhere else. But we've got to save Josh. Besides, I'll stop them before they get close to you."

"But I know judo."

"Of course. But you're the distraction, not the attacker."

"Because me beating them up won't distract them?"

Uncle David sighed.

She gave her uncle a hug.

He hugged her back. "Be careful, Abby."

She nodded and hopped over a log. Skirting rocks and scrub oaks, she ran toward the car.

After climbing the rope, then hiking across to the water-fall and climbing down to search for the film, then climbing back up, and finally this sprint to find cover—she wasn't a bit tired.

She would save Josh.

Now that she was out of the mobsters' view, she charged behind the boulders and tore for the black car. Heat bounced off the metal like a frying pan. She lowered her sleeve over her hand and flung open the door, leapt inside, and tugged the door closed.

Thank God she'd watched her uncle drive. She glanced at the array of glass dials, levers, and pedals. If he could drive, she could drive.

She sat on the seat's edge, flipped the ignition switch and stamped her left foot on the clutch and her right onto the starter. The engine roared to life.

A thrill shot through her as the motor vibrations hummed along her spine. In no time, the smell of exhaust filled the car through the open windows. The fear that had lodged in her chest turned to giggles. Josh hated it when she started giggling, but she couldn't help it.

Keeping her foot on the clutch so the car wouldn't move, she stamped hard on the gas pedal. The engine roared and the car shook. Surely the mobsters heard the noise.

She let off the gas, then punched the accelerator again, and the engine howled. She leaned forward and bumped the gearshift.

A terrible grinding noise filled the car, then stopped. The wheels spun in the sand and found a grip. She grabbed the wheel at the same instant the car burst from behind the rocks like a cannonball. She cranked the steering wheel just in time to avoid a small tree. The other side of the car nearly lifted from the ground. Her heart jumped in her throat.

She straightened the vehicle and found herself hurtling directly at the mobsters—*and her brother*. The car bounced over rocks and gravel, down small dips and over mounds.

Through the dusty windshield, she looked past the radiator cap and hood ornament to three men in black suits with Josh. They all stared at her, but they didn't move.

If they thought just because she was a girl and could barely see over the steering column that she wouldn't run them over, they'd better think again.

They pointed guns at her brother. She'd stop them.

She stamped harder on the gas pedal.

Josh acted first. He ran away, in the direction of the trees where Uncle David hid.

The mobsters caught Josh before he'd gone far.

It was then she saw Uncle David closing in on the men from behind, a large branch in his hand.

CHAPTER FOURTEEN
May, 1925
Havasupai Trailhead

*J*osh dropped to a knee as Abby sped by. The mobsters stood over him, and the boss lowered his gun, pointing toward Abby.

Then Josh saw his uncle racing up from behind.

Abby and the car had turned and were racing toward them again.

A thick branch gripped in his hands, Uncle David charged toward the men just as the car roared by, spraying dirt and barely missing the mobsters, who scrambled through the cloud of dust.

Behind them, Josh's uncle raised the branch high over his head and brought it down on the short mobster's head with a hollow thud that Josh heard over the rumble of the car engine.

The man dropped to his knees and fell face first into the sand. Uncle David kicked away his gun.

The boss swung his machine gun at Uncle David, who jumped out of the way, easily dodging the blow. With a shout, his uncle kicked the barrel hard, and the deadly machine gun spun through the air, crashing on a rock, then bouncing into Abby's path. The car's tires smashed the weapon.

Josh lowered his shoulder and rammed into the boss's stomach. He fell, gasping for breath.

"Josh," yelled his uncle. "Run to the car!"

Before he could follow his uncle's orders, the strong man aimed his gun at Uncle David, who slowly lifted his hands.

Could his uncle take on someone whose muscles made his suit look too small?

Abby raced by, and when the dust cleared enough to see, the strong man's gun lay on the ground, and he was throw-

ing a punch at Uncle David. His uncle ducked, and gave the strong man an uppercut.

The mobster fell back, his nose bleeding.

Josh saw movement at the mobster's feet. A Gila monster! Perfect timing.

The mobster kicked at the creature that thumped against his boot.

The Gila monster hissed and bit the man's leg. He yelled, scrambled to his feet, and hopped on one leg and kicked the leg with the venomous lizard attached, but the Gila monster held on tight.

"Go Josh," Uncle David called. "I'll take care of this one."

Josh nodded, saw one man unconscious, the second still trying to breathe, and the third fighting the Gila monster attached to his leg. Josh started toward the cloud of dust that was Abby.

As Josh ran by him, Uncle David knocked the man over the head, and he fell, Gila monster still clinging tight.

Abby slowed the car, and Josh reached to catch the back-door handle. He jumped onto the running board, and dove through the window. He fell onto the backseat in a heap.

"Abby, quick, pick up Uncle David!"

As Josh righted himself, he saw the boss recover, reach into his jacket pocket, and pull out a knife. Uncle David lowered a shoulder and slammed into his side. The mobster crashed to the sand, and both rolled.

Abby swerved the car around a bush and aimed directly for Uncle David.

The mobster jumped up and slashed his knife at their uncle again and again. Uncle David ducked, then swung the heavy satchel filled with tools, hitting the man in the midsection. The man doubled over, and Uncle David swung a left hook at his jaw. The mobster stumbled and landed against a cactus. He let out a long, loud howl and fell to the ground.

"Did you see that?" Josh pounded the seatback. "Uncle David just nailed that guy!"

Abby stomped on the brake and Josh rolled against the front seat and fell to the floor. Their uncle opened the driver's door, and Abby said, "I'll drive."

Uncle David trotted alongside the car as it rolled slowly forward. "Abby, scoot over."

"I'm a good driver."

Uncle David jumped in as she reluctantly slid to the passenger side.

"Wait," the strong man shouted. "Help me!" He took a stick and tried to beat the lizard off his leg. "I'm going to die!"

"You won't die," Josh said as they passed by. "It'll just make you kinda sick."

Abby yelled, "They're coming! Uncle David, go, go, go!"

Josh saw the other five, along with the round Slim, coming out of the side ravine. Over the rumble of the motor, they heard the rattle of a tommy gun. To Josh's relief, they were too far away, and the shots missed.

Uncle David gripped the wheel, let off the clutch, and slammed his foot down. Josh flew back in his seat as they charged across the desert toward the road. He righted himself, glanced behind them, and saw only dust.

Uncle David put the car into third gear and yelled above the engine's roar, "We have to get to the airplane—fast."

Josh nodded. "Right." He checked behind him, and saw the men racing toward the vehicles.

"Can we tell the police?" Abby asked.

Uncle David shook his head. "Tell them that we're being chased by mobsters? That we fought them off?" He shook his head again. "We don't know who we can trust. What if the mobsters paid them off? Let's get to the plane and get home."

Uncle David turned onto the main road, and they picked up speed.

He rubbed his knuckles and sighed. He glanced at Abby. "Good job. But I don't want to see you driving again until you're at least Josh's age. Got it?"

She reached into her pocket and pulled out a small tin. She shook the canister and the film inside rattled.

She gave a triumphant shout, and Josh and Uncle David joined her.

Josh jumped out of the car, skidded to a halt in front of the airplane, and tossed his bag into the front cockpit.

"Josh. I forgot, we're out of charges to start the engine." Uncle David chucked his satchel into the plane. "Crawl in and open the throttle about half a finger's width and activate the magnetos. Then pull the lever on the left. I'll spin the propeller."

Josh crawled over the side of the rear cockpit and fell into the seat. Abby clambered into the front cockpit. "Hey!" she called. "They're coming!"

With no time to look, Josh tugged the small knob. With the throttle open, he pulled on the magneto. The lever aligned the magnets in the motor. He flipped the ignition switch. Josh thanked God that his father had let him tinker with car motors so he knew how this worked.

He glanced over the cockpit's edge at his uncle.

Uncle David reached up and grabbed the propeller. He hesitated, then yanked down with all his might.

A distant plume of dust caught Josh's attention as the engine popped to life and dust and exhaust filled the air. He could make out a car, the same make the mobsters drove.

Josh was tempted to start the aircraft forward as Uncle David put a foot into the notch in the fuselage.

The main gravel road was about twenty feet away, with the farmer's house on one side of the plane, the barn on the other. The car sped closer on the gravel road.

"Stop!" Abby yelled over the noise of the coughing engine. "I can't find the film canister! I must have dropped it in the car!"

Uncle David glanced at the oncoming car and hollered, "Josh, can you taxi to the road?"

"I just pull the throttle to move forward, right?"

"Right." Uncle David jumped from the plane and raced for the farmer's car.

Josh tugged on the throttle and the plane strained forward. The engine grew louder. He pulled the throttle out more...nothing. A little farther, and the plane rocked back and forth. The propeller was spinning fast. Was he supposed to open the gas all the way? Uncle David was nearing the car. But the mobster's vehicle was almost to the farm. Josh could see the boss driving, and four locals in the back.

He yanked hard on the lever and the engine roared. The plane bounced and jostled over the blocks they'd placed in front of the tires. It jerked forward, then rolled toward the road, gaining speed. Josh's heart leapt into his throat.

Abby screamed and pointed at the approaching car, but the engine noise prevented him from hearing what she said.

He pushed the throttle back, and the engine almost died. He set the lever to a calm taxi, but they sped onto the main road. He tugged the stick to the left, and they bounced off the gravel road and into the ditch, then back onto the road. The wings rocked back and forth.

The car barreled straight for them and almost clipped their wing before turning at the last second. Three mobsters peered at them as the car raced by.

Josh glanced behind him. Uncle David was running to catch up. But the mobster's car spun around and gave chase.

He slowed enough for Uncle David to catch up. The car veered toward his uncle, and he jumped out of the way. The car drove close to the left wing.

Josh angled the plane toward the car. The wing tapped the windshield and the car spun away, lurched into the ditch, flipped over, and landed on its roof with a crash. Josh craned his neck to watch the mobsters pull themselves out the windows.

Uncle David sprinted past the car.

The boss started running right behind Uncle David, and the mobster was fast.

Josh slowed the airplane. Their enemies were catching up, but Josh needed to give his uncle a chance to grab onto the plane. He kept the aircraft in the center of the road and turned his head again to see Uncle David sprinting along the gravel.

How much energy did his uncle have left in him?

Abby yelled, "Come on, Uncle David, you can do it."

Uncle David lowered his head, pumped his arms. He ran so fast, dust flew off his jacket.

Abby pointed ahead. *Another* car was coming at them.

She looked back and screamed over the thrum of the engine and the crunch of gravel. "Uncle David!"

Josh turned. The slim man was almost close enough to touch him.

Josh slowed the plane even more. His uncle grabbed the lip of the cockpit. His legs pounded on the gravel. But the man grasped his sleeve.

Josh sped up and the mobster lost his grip.

Josh grabbed his uncle's arm.

The car was coming at them fast. A man leaned out the window, a tommy gun aimed their direction.

With a loud yell, Uncle David swung a leg up and caught his toe in the tiny step. "Punch it, Josh!" He hung tight to the outside of the airplane.

Josh yanked on the throttle. The engine thrummed and wind rushed through his hair.

"He's got my leg!" Uncle David gripped the cockpit with one hand, and with a full-body right jab, sent the gangster flying into the dirt.

Flipping his legs up and over the lip, he wedged in beside Josh. "Scoot. I need to reach the rudder pedals."

Josh slid over as far as he could. The plane gained speed, but the car was going to ram them!

Uncle David grasped the stick. "Can't rise too soon or we'll stall."

The plane bounced straight for the oncoming car. The tommy gun and its owner leaned farther out the window and pointed the gun at them. They were almost within range.

Josh saw the wide eyes of the driver.

"Duck!" Uncle David shouted.

He pulled back on the stick. Josh gripped his head as the

plane lifted from the ground. The vibration from the gravel road stopped as they soared into the air. Josh looked over the edge. The plane's wheels almost hit the car as it passed underneath.

Uncle David raised a fist. "Yeah!" Then he yelled, "Get down!"

Josh heard bullets punching through the light metal and fabric. But the plane continued to rise. He looked over the edge of the cockpit again and saw tiny holes in the wing. He glanced down at the man pointing his gun at them. But no more pings.

In front of them, Abby took off her pith helmet, pulled on the goggles, and turned. The wind whipped her ponytail to one side. "They'll have men waiting for us at the airport," she yelled above the engine noise.

Uncle David looked over the edge of the cockpit, then cupped a hand to the side of his mouth. "We'll land in Colbey, not Nashville. We can pick up the car later."

Josh stared down at the mobster boss, who was already a tiny, toy-like figure far below. The man lowered his gun. Josh couldn't help but sigh with relief.

The wind carried Abby's voice. "Did you get the film, Uncle David?"

He grinned, reached into his jacket pocket and pulled out the tin. Abby lifted both hands in celebration and sank back into her seat, out of sight. Josh had a feeling she'd either fall asleep or pull a book out of her bag.

"The trouble you two can find…" Uncle David shook his head and laughed.

"But we did it. We got away!" Josh yelled at the top of his lungs.

They were all hot and sweaty and beyond exhausted, but Josh didn't mind. After all they'd been through together, he had a lot to think about. Having someone to talk with for a while might be nice.

His uncle had really gone the distance with them.

Josh stared up at the bottom of the cloud they were passing under. He had to shout to be heard. "Someone really wants to stop us from proving that dinosaurs and men lived together."

"Something's up...that's for sure." His uncle rubbed his stubbled chin. "But this whole mess has been a lot of trouble for...what?" He reached to the floor and picked up a set of goggles.

"The Scopes trial you've been talking about." Josh set his hat on the floor and ran his fingers through his hair. He shouted, "Do you think it's them? The defendants?"

"Surely not." David lowered his brow and shook his head. For a moment, he kept his gaze on the empty sky in front of them. Finally, he pulled his goggles on. "Give me some time to think and make sense of things. What we saw in the canyon doesn't fit my evolutionary thought. At all."

Josh took a deep breath and looked his uncle in the eye. "You're a good fighter. The way you hit that guy... You singlehandedly took out three men in a matter of minutes, maybe seconds. Incredible!" He adjusted his goggles.

David clapped him on the back. "You're a fighter too, Josh! Your quick thinking got us out of more than one predicament."

Josh glowed inside. He was in the plane with one of the leading biologists in the country, who happened to be his uncle...and that man was proud of him.

Uncle David checked the controls, then turned to Josh. "I've read Dr. Hubbard's preliminary report. I thought his finds were made up, that the drawings and the prints weren't real. Seeing them in person, I know they're real. But Dr. Hubbard thinks evidence proves that man has been on the earth a lot longer ago than current theories allow. As long as a million years. What do you think, Josh?"

Josh appreciated that his uncle asked for his opinion, but he thought carefully about how he should answer. Sometimes, talking about his beliefs about creation had made people angry. Instead, he asked a question. "Could the evidence mean that dinosaurs didn't go extinct as long ago as some scientists suggest? Maybe, dinosaurs are only six or eight thousand years old?"

"What?" his uncle yelled over the wind. "I thought you said eight thousand."

"I did!"

Uncle David was quiet for a while. Finally, he said, "Instead of humans being old, maybe dinosaurs are young. Maybe."

Josh settled in his corner of the seat and watched the flimsy clouds whiz by around them, almost within reach. A darkness settled over his heart. *Why?* he wondered. Why was he suddenly feeling a little melancholy?

Because he'd almost failed Uncle David and Abby today. He hadn't been strong enough to climb the rope.

"Hey, Josh," Uncle David shouted.

He looked up at his uncle. "Yeah?"

"You're quite the thinker." He squeezed Josh's shoulder. "We were in quite a pickle, and you found a way to warn us about those men before we got there. Great job."

Josh grinned. As soon as the film was developed, they could prove to the world that dinosaurs and humans lived together. His uncle was considering creation as a possible scientific explanation for the origins of the world. Their adventures had been fantastic. But best of all, Uncle David was proud of him.

Now, what exactly would the film show?

CHAPTER FIFTEEN
May, 1925 - Eleven Hours Later
Colbey, Tennessee

*J*osh used the flashlight to illuminate the cockpit and check on Abby.

She sat up as the engine shut off and the propeller came to a halt. "Are we home?"

"Yeah."

"That was fast."

"Tailwinds from the west. We stopped a couple times to fuel." Josh unfastened his harness, then helped Abby with hers. "I thought I'd better ride with you."

She rubbed her head. "What time is it?"

"Four in the morning."

He held her hand as she felt for the foothold outside the plane, then crawled out himself. The air was far warmer down here, but he still kept his jacket around him. His canteen strap was still wrapped over his shoulder, the round tin container hanging by his side. He left it there as they waited for Uncle David to finish inside the plane.

The lane was lit by electric streetlights, where houses lined the road. On the opposite side of the street, Josh remembered fields. It was a black void, now.

Porchlights popped on, and several men hurried over to check on the commotion.

"We're fine," Uncle David said as he stepped out of the cockpit. "Going to sleep, then we'll take the plane the rest of the way to Nashville after school."

The neighbors helped push the plane into the field, and Uncle David blocked the wheels.

"Sure you're all right, Dr. Hunter?" one man asked, shining his flashlight down to show his rumpled and torn archeology clothes.

"Never better. Thanks, Harry."

The three of them stumbled to the nearby college, walking down the empty street in the middle of the night.

"When does the drugstore open so we can develop the pictures?" Abby asked.

Uncle David pointed the flashlight's beam on the ground in front of them. "There's a dark room in the biology building. We will know everything those pictures have to tell in thirty minutes."

Josh's legs would barely move. He'd walked or run nearly

twenty miles. Only a few times in his life had he ever gone that far in one day.

Uncle David fumbled with the keys to the biology building's front door and, finally, the lock clicked. They stepped into the long, dimly lit hallway. The only light came from the street lamps outside. The stuffed animals, butterfly collection, and dinosaur bones lurking in the shadows made the hair on Josh's neck stand up. He wasn't afraid they would come to life. They were just…eerie.

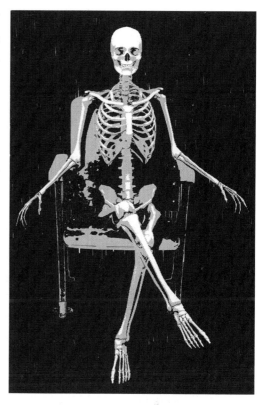

Hurrying past the grizzly bear, they stepped into Uncle David's classroom. He snapped on a desk lamp that illuminated his nameplate: *Dr. David Hunter*. Josh turned to the rows of seats veiled by darkness and saw a skeleton, sitting in the front row. He yelled and jumped back. Abby screamed.

"It's okay, it's fine." Uncle David reached to steady them, laughing. "Some of my students put it there, no doubt. Almost every time I walk in, it's in a different place." He set his bag on the desk.

Josh clutched his hammering heart. "Scared me." He dropped his bag as well.

"Me, too," Abby whispered. She looked pale, even in the darkness.

"I've gotten used to seeing it pop up here and there." Uncle David crossed to the front row and picked up the bones by the shoulders. "Come on, Mortimer. Back to your stand."

"You named him?" Abby asked.

"Yep. Mortimer." He set the bones on the wire hanger. "Once, he was propped on my desk like he owned the place. Another time, he was half out the window, as if trying to escape." He opened his satchel and pulled out the canister. "I'm going to go develop the film first thing. We need to see what's on it before anyone knows we're back. We bought some time, I think. But we need to know what you two have." He raised a brow. "And don't think I forgot what you said about Professor Thomas. If he shows up on here…" He held up the canister.

As Uncle David walked out the door, Abby said, "I wish he'd taken us with him. I've always wanted to see inside a darkroom—and that skeleton gives me the creeps."

Josh shrugged. "You can't see in a darkroom. And Mortimer can't hurt us."

Abby sat behind the desk and took off her pith helmet. Josh watched as she tapped on it for a few moments, sending a hollow thump echoing through the room. Then she crossed her arms, set them on the desk, and buried her face in them. She let loose a long breath and let her lips flutter, making a motor sound. "How long now?"

"He just left."

She slumped in the chair. She looked at the ceiling and took a deep breath. "'Will you walk a little faster?' said a whiting to a snail. 'There's a porpoise close behind us, and he's treading on my tail.'"

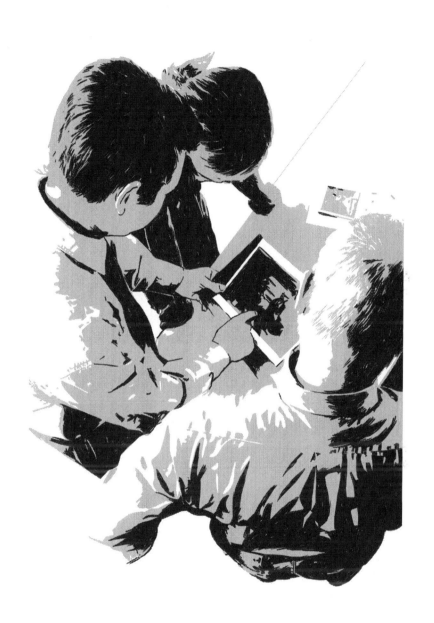

Josh listened as she quoted *The Lobster Quadrille* from Lewis Caroll's *Alice in Wonderland,* and when she finished, she switched to nursery rhymes.

"I brought one." The door opened and Uncle David appeared, fanning a photograph in the air. "The other prints are still drying." He waved the picture for a few moments. Finally, he laid the print on the desk, under the lamp.

Josh sat in his uncle's chair and studied the picture in the light. "It's blurry."

"The heat's damaged the film." David leaned over the picture. "It's probably only the waterfall that kept it cool enough to see this much."

"I can't believe this." Josh squinted at the black-and-white photograph, seeing only gray shadows and vague figures.

"I'll get the others. They should be dry by now." When his uncle returned several minutes later, Josh got up so his uncle could sit at the desk. "We can see the photos better with more light."

Uncle David spread the pictures out on the desktop and positioned the lamp so the light focused directly over the first photograph. He pulled a magnifying glass from a desk drawer and stared through it, mumbling to himself. After a bit, he glanced up at Josh. "These are the footprints?"

Josh pointed. "Coelophysis." He splayed out his fingers. "About the size of my hand."

"In the future, put something in the photo—like a coin or a ruler—so we can compare."

"I was in a hurry." But he had to admit that wasn't entirely true. The hoodlums hadn't entered the canyon until after he'd taken the picture. "Actually, I was so excited I forgot. That one, I'm pretty sure, is my knee. Abby bumped me a time or two."

Uncle David lowered the magnifying glass.

"Look at this one." Josh pointed again. "See how the animal prints are spaced far apart? The dinosaur was fast, very fast. We also saw several different-sized footprints."

Uncle David looked up from studying the pictures. "Different sized human prints?"

"Maybe. I think the Coelophysis were hunting in a pack. Here, this picture is the human footprint. It's clear here. And here's another of the spacing of the dinosaur tracks."

Uncle David leaned back in his chair. The squeak echoed in the empty room. "The photo of the dinosaur and human tracks together isn't focused enough. Too grainy. But I can see the outlines. You did good." He shook his head. "If it wasn't for the damaged film."

Josh picked up another picture. "Here are more paintings of ibex. Like you saw. And I think this could have been a painting of a dinosaur. The figure was a lot like the carvings we saw." He pointed at another picture. "I think this is the one of the men who destroyed the tracks."

Uncle David lowered the light and hovered his magnifying glass over the foggy print. "I can't tell who any of the men are. Dark clothes, I see. I think probably the mob."

Abby bent over the desk. "Can you see? Under this one's hat? His blond hair?"

He brought the magnifying glass closer. "Look you two. Does this man look like the one we pushed from the plane?"

Josh glanced at the photo. "Yes, that's the man they called *the boss*." He took the magnifying glass. "That one's *slim*. A joke, calling him slim, I think."

Abby grabbed Josh's arm and lowered her voice and glanced toward the door. "Did you hear that?"

Josh tilted his head. "The front door opening?"

Uncle David shook his head. "I didn't hear anything. You two are easily spooked tonight."

Abby looked from the doorway to the window behind them.

Josh followed Abby's gaze through the glass and into the inky darkness. Someone was out there. He could sense it, even if he couldn't see them.

"Heels," Abby whispered, turning back to the door."

A shadow crossed over the window in the door. Josh crouched, ready to leap behind a row of empty seats and pull Abby with him. The handle turned, and with a squeak, the door slowly opened. He glanced at Uncle David, who was now watching the door with a look of concern on his face. His uncle's hand grasped a glass paperweight on the desk.

Miss Emma stood in the doorway. "Goodness." Her warm smile turned to a concerned frown. "You three look like you've seen a ghost."

Uncle David laughed, relief in his voice. "For a minute there, I was wishing I had a frying pan handy."

She shot him a look, but her eyes were laughing too.

"I called Emma from the office while I grabbed the pictures," he explained to Josh and Abby.

He walked across the room and took Miss Emma in his arms. "I thought you said you couldn't come down for a bit?" He kissed her cheek.

"David," she said with a giggle. "The kids!"

Josh sighed. Adults.

"I missed you."

The moment he released his fiancée, Abby threw herself into Miss Emma's arms. "I missed you, too, Miss Emma, but we had such an adventure. Uncle David bought new clothes for the desert, and I climbed the cliffs. Six times, up and down. And I drove a car, all by myself."

"Goodness. You did all that?" Miss Emma put her arm around Abby and walked her over to the desk. To Josh's surprise, she hugged him, too. He smelled her lilac perfume and sensed strength.

"Josh, it's so good to see you again." She pulled him close.

He offered a shy smile, ashamed by how much he needed the hug.

"Josh sent ten men the wrong way so we could start the car and Uncle David could bonk the other men on the head, while we escaped." Abby nearly jumped up and down. "Oh, and a Gila monster bit one of them. After that, we took off in the airplane just before the bad guys started shooting. They put holes in the airplane, but it's okay, and we landed just a bit ago. I'm glad to be home." She snuggled against Emma.

Josh smiled. *Home.* Yes, this was their home now.

Miss Emma released the two of them and reached for David's scraped hand. "What happened, dear?"

He shrugged. "Things got a little rough."

"Oh, David..."

Abby punched the air with one fist, then the other. "Uncle David knocked out the boss before getting on the plane. *Bam-bam.*"

"Three men with tommy guns," Josh said, "but Uncle David fought them all off."

Miss Emma gasped and her face paled.

Uncle David took her elbow. "Perhaps you should sit and we can start at the beginning."

"I'm okay." Miss Emma lifted an eyebrow. "New clothes,

David?"

He looked at his dusty leather jacket. "Not my usual, I admit."

She smiled. "You definitely look ducky." She glanced at the desk. "I take it you retrieved the film. Are these the pictures?"

"They're too blurry to tell what's really going on," Abby said, "but we think we've narrowed down the identity of two of the men."

Josh pointed them out. "Slim and the Boss. And a third one, Professor—"

Uncle David cleared his throat, cutting Josh off. "Like I said, we should probably start at the beginning."

"Later." she straightened, yawning. "For now, I'm glad you're all home safe and your archeology adventures are over."

Outside, the sun crept over the horizon. But something in Josh's gut told him their adventures were just beginning.

CHAPTER SIXTEEN
May, 1925 - Six Hours Later
Colbey, Tennessee

*J*osh couldn't sleep. He'd been lying on his bed for an hour since they got home, but his mind refused to slow down. It didn't help that outside his window, the sun was high in the sky. And it didn't help that a Carolina chickadee chirped out front, calling out to the world the front yard belonged to him.

He needed to *do* something. Finally, he tossed back the covers and sat up.

He wandered into the front room, rubbing his face. Uncle

David and Miss Emma sat on the couch, holding hands.

"Josh?" Concern etched his uncle's face.

"I can't sleep. I want to jog. Get into shape."

"What's wrong?" Miss Emma asked. "Aren't you feeling well?"

"I'm out of shape. I couldn't keep up with Abby and Uncle David." He looked at the floor. Failure was a hard thing to admit.

"I'm not sure I want you out there by yourself. Bad guys and all..." His uncle leaned forward, hands clasped on his knees.

"Just around the block? Please... I can't sleep...my mind won't let me. Look, it's a beautiful day, the weather's perfect. Let me go around the block, and you can watch me through the window."

Uncle David took a long breath, then nodded. "All right. But as you run, go slow enough so you enough energy to sprint back."

Josh returned to his room, stripped off his pajama shirt, then paused when he heard Miss Emma say, "David, you asked a mechanic to call about your brother's car? I received a phone call from Arizona. A man said something about an accident."

Josh pulled on a white t-shirt. When he heard crying, he stepped closer to his door and reached for the doorknob. He would comfort her if he could.

He paused when she continued.

"He said skid from the tires showed that the car swerved before hitting the tree." She sobbed. "Oh David, I thought he was talking about you and the children! I thought... Oh, it was so awful. I thought you'd all been in an automobile accident. Finally, the man explained it wasn't you, and told me what you'd asked him to do."

"I'm so sorry, Emma. I'm so, so sorry. When I asked him to call you, I never once thought you'd think it was us he was talking about. Of course he was talking about my brother—about Peter and Mary who were in the car wreck."

"I don't know what I'd do if I lost you."

Josh wanted to go tell Miss Emma that everything would be okay. He'd lost people he loved. You just moved on the best you could, with the help of God and others you loved and who loved you. And with that thought, Josh realized how much he'd changed the past few days.

"David…" Miss Emma's voice was a whisper. Josh pressed his ear against the door. "The mechanic said the brake lines were cut, not broken. It was a clean cut."

Anger ripped through Josh's chest. It was one thing to *suspect* his parents had been purposely killed, but another to have that suspicion confirmed.

After a long pause, Uncle David spoke again. "I'll admit, Josh has me rethinking my beliefs about Earth's origins. My brother tried to convince me more than once, and I would argue with him. But I saw things, Emma. Evidences that cannot be ignored. And I saw interpretations of facts through Josh and Abby's eyes, children's eyes, that were simple and easy to understand. Not long, complicated discussions that muddle facts and twist views." He groaned. "And I wrote a book that does just that."

Josh got off the bed, slipped out of his pajama bottoms and into a pair of knee-length knickerbockers.

Emma laughed. "And to think you've been asked to testify in the Scopes trial."

"I'm glad you think it's funny." David grunted. "I'm not sure what I'll say."

Josh tied his shoes and opened his door. Uncle David stood, rubbing his beat-up knuckles. "Have fun, Josh. My lunch break is over in half an hour, so I may be at school when you get back.

Josh stepped into the sunny day and ran onto the sidewalk. His footsteps pounding the concrete and his loud breathing beat a pattern in his head. A car buzzed by, and he thought about the stupidity of jogging. He wasn't going anywhere. Just running a loop around the block.

And then another loop.

One section of sidewalk slanted upward. He jumped over the crack. Around the corner, a massive cottonwood tree blocked the sun, and a root shot up through the sidewalk to tilt the concrete.

He passed Uncle David's house and almost stopped. Running felt so useless. But thinking about how he'd deserted Abby and Uncle David in the canyon kept him running. He'd be ready for their next adventure.

Sweat ran down his neck and temples, but he didn't falter. One more time, he jumped the sidewalk gap, skirted the cottonwood roots.

When he approached his uncle's house again, he doubled over with pain. Holding his side, he tried to breathe. The stitch in his side made him feel like his stomach would fall out. His lungs were about to explode.

You can do this, he told himself. *Just one more lap.* He pulled his wet shirt away from his skin.

In an attempt to divert his mind from his screaming muscles, he tried to think of a solution to their latest problem.

They needed the mobsters to know there was nothing on the pictures, that they were grainy—too foggy to make anything out. Then maybe the bad guys would leave them alone.

Step by step, sidewalk square by sidewalk square, an idea formed in his head. He'd come across a word a few days ago that fit what he was thinking—one he'd looked up in the dictionary. *Counterintuitive*. Something that didn't agree with what seemed true. Giving the pictures to the mobsters seemed counterintuitive, but after thinking through the problem, he was convinced that losing the pictures was the best way to get the gangsters off their backs.

The question was, how to proceed?

He stumbled over a crack in the sidewalk.

They couldn't just walk up to the villains and say, "Here are the pictures. We don't want them anymore." The mobsters might think they'd made duplicates for themselves. Somehow, they had to get the negatives and pictures into the hands of the men who'd almost killed for them, and then convince them there were no duplicates.

He jumped over the tree roots.

He slowed down and his side cramped as he rounded the next corner.

He stopped, bent over, breathing hard. He was done.

Hands on hips, he leaned against Uncle David's picket fence, and an idea popped in his head. One that would give them a chance to convince the mobsters there were no duplicates, let them have the photos, and the best part, there was even a chance they could capture a mobster so the police could question him.

That was the dangerous part of his plan.

CHAPTER SEVENTEEN
May, 1925 - One Minute Later
Colbey, Tennessee

Abby woke to sound of piano music. The beautiful tune was the saddest song she'd ever heard. She rubbed her eyes and crawled out of bed. The worst part about taking a morning nap was that she usually felt strange afterward. Fog filled her head and her eyes were puffy. She didn't have to look in a mirror to know that. She shook her head to clear the cobwebs. Had all her recent adventures been only a dream?

She wandered down the hall and into the living room. Uncle David sat on the piano bench, his hands running up and down the keys. He'd apparently showered and dressed for school. His suit jacket lay beside him on the bench. He looked up from the piano, startled. "Oh, Abby, I'm sorry. I didn't mean to wake you. I was on my lunch break and I forgot you were asleep. Miss Emma was here earlier, and when she left, I started playing."

Pounding footsteps were followed by the sound of the door flying open. Abby spun around in time to see Josh burst in the front door.

Uncle David jumped up and the piano bench crashed against the wood floor. "Josh, what's wrong?"

Her brother held up a hand, obviously trying to catch his breath.

"Is someone following you?" Uncle David hurried to the door.

Josh shook his head.

Abby cocked her head. "You have an idea."

He nodded.

Abby swallowed. "You've got to stop doing that, Josh. You scare me every time."

"A trap." He took a deep breath. "We need to set a trap."

"What are you talking about?"

He wiped sweat from his face with his t-shirt. "We need to get those pictures to the mobsters, so they'll think we've lost our proof that humans and dinosaurs lived at the same time. Then they'll leave us alone." He took another breath. "But we need to know who is behind this, so…we set a trap. If they go for the pictures and escape—great. They leave us alone after that."

"But…" Hope danced in Abby's heart. "If we capture them as they go for the bait…"

"Then the police can question them and find out who's behind all this." Josh ran his fingers through his damp hair.

Uncle David righted the piano bench then re-tucked his shirt and hitched up his pants. "Good idea, Josh. Really, it is. But how do you plan to pull it off? And what's to convince them we won't make copies?"

Josh's face lit up. "Tonight. Tell the Darwin Club there's a special meeting, and I'll discuss what we discovered on the Doheny Expedition, and what Dr. Hubbard found. Now, this part is important. Let the story get around that I have photos that prove man and dinosaurs lived together.

"Once I'm done, I'll ask what I should do with them. You tell me to leave them on the desk, that they should be okay there overnight. I'll ask you, 'even the negatives?' You say, 'Yes.' Then, once the students look at them, they'll pass the word around that the pictures are too foggy to see. I'm guessing the mobsters will want the pictures anyway. And then we wait for a thief to come into the school, look for duplicates, and we nab him. Or he'll get away with the photos. Either way, it works."

Uncle David picked up his suit jacket and dusted off the sleeves. "How can you be sure someone at the meeting will report our little exchange to the mobsters?"

Josh slumped against the wall and took a deep breath. "I think Professor Thomas might be giving information to them. That's how they got Dad's letter—I think he stole it from Dr. Michaels. Someone at the college must be helping them. It's the only thing that makes sense."

Uncle David glanced at his watch. "I have just enough time to check with the police before my first class begins. We can have them stake out the Biology Building." He straightened. "Josh, I'm a bit surprised you volunteered to stand in front of college students and speak. Are you sure about this?"

"I'll be okay."

But when Abby caught his expression, it seemed like what he was really saying was, "What have I gotten myself in for?"

Uncle David put on his jacket. "Go ahead, prepare for tonight. But you'll be speaking before college students. They're a tough crowd. You've got to be convincing. Can you do it?"

"Yeah, I think so." He wiped new sweat from his forehead. Abby couldn't decide if it was nerves or from his run. The last time Josh had been at a Darwin Club meeting, he'd run away after that rude student called him fatso.

"Do you have all the material you need, Josh? This is a college class. I've plenty of books here."

"Yes." He wiped his brow again. "I can teach." His voice squeaked. And he groaned.

Abby shook her head. If his voice did that tonight, he wouldn't convince anyone.

"All right then, I'll check with police. Then I'll pass the word at school that we have a guest speaker who believes he has proof that humans and dinosaurs walked the earth at the same time. He has photos to prove his position. But Josh, I have to tell you, this crowd knows evolution. You've got to know what you're talking about."

Josh swallowed. "I'll do my best."

"You'll need to look spiffy, too." Abby headed for the kitchen. "I'm hungry." At the door, she called over her shoulder, "We've got to find you some nice clothes."

"I've got nice clothes."

"And a shower wouldn't hurt either."

Uncle David laughed. "I'll see if Miss Emma can get away

from the office to take you shopping this afternoon." He reached for his cup that sat on the piano, and took a sip of coffee. "Fred said he would fly the plane to Nashville, since he was heading that way anyway, and he will drive the car back for us." He set his cup down. "I'd better run down to the police station. Be ready tonight. Meet me in my classroom at four o'clock sharp.

Josh set another of Uncle David's books on his desk by his bedroom door, open to the section he wanted. That made five books now that separated humans and dinosaurs in different eras.

He glanced at his new clothes hanging on the closet knob. Miss Emma had promised a soda after shopping, so he'd picked out the first clothes he tried on, enjoyed the soda, and then come home to prepare for his talk.

Miss Emma and Abby sat on the couch in the living room, talking and laughing. He wished they'd be quiet. After all, they knew he was trying to study. This wasn't for a mere school exam. This was serious life-and-death stuff. He was trying to get the mobsters on a different track and save all their lives.

"You have beautiful hair, Abby."

He looked through the door and into the living room. Miss Emma was brushing his sister's long, blond tresses. "But you simply arrange it in a ponytail. I must tell you…no one wears ponytails anymore, dear."

"But we're always in a hurry."

"I know, but for those moments when there's time, have a

little fun with different styles now and again. You're too pretty to hide behind a ponytail."

Ugh. Why couldn't they be quiet? But he didn't bother getting up to close the door.

Twenty minutes later, after he'd stopped listening, Josh glanced up. His sister looked completely different. A golden braid crowned her head.

"Looks nice, Abby," he called.

She giggled. "Thanks, Josh."

The phone rang. Miss Emma jumped to her feet and ran to the wall. She picked up the earpiece, and after a moment, held the phone to Josh. "It's your uncle."

He hurried into the living room. "The plan is on, Josh." Uncle David's voice sounded tinny over the phone line. "I got two police deputies to help us tonight. Wasn't hard to convince them since we had the break-in at the house."

"Thanks. See you in a bit." Josh set the handle on the plunger and turned to his sister. "He said the police will help us tonight."

"Do you think it'll be dangerous, though?"

"Yeah, Abby. This'll be dangerous."

She clapped. "Oh, good."

Miss Emma sighed.

CHAPTER EIGHTEEN
May, 1925 - One Hour Later
Colbey College

Abby stood beside her uncle just inside his classroom doorway and watched students file inside. She smiled at them as they walked by. Row by row, they filled the one-hundred-and-fifty seats that rose from the front to the back of the room.

The Darwin Club had sixty members, but today, every seat was filled.

Students stuffed their book bags under their seats and professors sat along the front row with amused looks on their faces and spectacles low on their noses. The room buzzed with conversation.

Abby swallowed. They were about to hear a lecture from a thirteen-year-old boy. How would they respond?

She peeked through the doorway again. Josh had gone to the bathroom for the third time, just before the classroom began to fill. Now, he was about to be late.

Miss Emma stood on Abby's left. Professor Thomas, who sat in the front row, smiled at Miss Emma, who glanced at Uncle David before returning the smile.

Uncle David, on Abby's right, cleared his throat, obviously unhappy with the exchange, then he turned back to Dr. Michaels to continue a debate. They kept their voices low.

Uncle David had filled Emma's father in on the plan.

"I'll allow your nephew to give his opinion on the origins of the universe," Dr. Michaels said, "but to have my daughter and the children risk their lives—"

"Emma is taking them back to my place for the night."

"Well, I'm glad you have the police here."

Abby had wanted to be a part of the stakeout. Uncle David had seen them in action, but he seemed just as eager as Dr. Michaels to keep them from getting in on the adventure.

Josh's setup for the talk was simple—a large drawing of a Coelophysis on an easel and a file on Uncle David's desk filled with photos and negatives.

She didn't see a single person in the audience who looked like a mobster.

"Perhaps I should go check on Josh," Uncle David said. "I'll be right back."

Emma leaned over to whisper, "I hope he's all right."

The feather in Miss Emma's hat tickled Abby's nose. She

sneezed just as Josh stepped into the room. He glanced at the full classroom and then at Abby, his eyes wide. His Adam's apple bounced up and down as he swallowed.

Standing by the door, Abby rubbed her sweaty palms together and tried to give him an encouraging smile.

There were so many students in the room now, that several had to stand along the walls and windows.

Josh plopped into a chair. His legs felt like noodles, or maybe jellyfish arms, which brought to mind an encyclopedia entry that said many scientists believed jellyfish were around during the time of the dinosaurs. Of course, Josh understood that jellyfish had existed when dinosaurs lived on the earth, just like humans did.

A surge of purpose filled him, diminishing the fear. But his hands still shook. Josh chewed his lip and prayed he didn't drop anything during his talk.

Uncle David stepped up to the wooden podium beside the desk and said a few words, but Josh was too nervous to listen. Finally, his uncle took a step back and motioned him forward. The sound of clapping reverberated between the walls.

He heard someone say, "He's just a kid."

Josh picked up the leather portfolio his uncle had loaned him and stepped to the podium. He set the folder on the desk, picked up the glass of water Miss Emma had placed there, and took a sip. Immediately he wished he hadn't. He couldn't stop his hands from shaking, and he was sure everyone could see the water sloshing around. He set the glass back on the desk, knocking it noisily against the podium, and rubbed his hands together.

Pulling several documents from the portfolio, he set them on the narrow lectern. The room quieted. Josh glanced at Abby, and she have him a thumbs up.

Josh grinned and turned to his audience. "Good evening." Despite his intention to sound authoritative, his voice sounded like he'd swallowed a lemon. He cleared his throat. "Good evening. My name is Josh Hunter. Welcome to the Darwin Club."

Generous applause filled the room, which for some reason, made him even more nervous.

Josh swallowed and gripped the podium.

Still at the door, Abby twisted a curl of hair that had escaped her braid, wrapping it round and round her finger. Miss Emma, whose hands were clasped in front of her, smiled. But Uncle David's jaw was tense. He looked ready to jump to the rescue, in the event Josh blew it.

Josh took a deep breath, dropped his shoulders and dove in. "Earlier this year," he said, "a man named Mr. Doheny donated money so that Dr. Samuel Hubbard and a large crew of men and one woman, my mom, could go to the Arizona desert to investigate sandstone carvings and dinosaur prints reported by locals. My parents were members of the expedition, and they took me and my sister with them. That's Abby, my sister, standing by my Uncle Da— Professor Hunter." Josh used the diversion to lick his dry lips.

He leaned forward. "While we were there, the team took photos and made casts of the carvings and the dinosaur tracks." He lifted the cup and swallowed another gulp of water. "Long ago, someone—or maybe several people carved elephants, dinosaurs, and ibex into the canyon walls. They were beautiful renditions and I felt privileged to be able to see something most people will never get to see."

A murmur of appreciation rippled through the room.

"Sight unseen, some scientists would suggest those carvings are hundreds of thousands or maybe even millions of years old."

Two of the professors nodded.

"But based on the evidence I saw there, I believe the drawings are eight-thousand years old—or less."

The students sat up, many looked at each other, shaking their heads. One professor rolled his eyes. Professor Thomas sat without moving. Not even a finger.

"You don't know what you're talking about," a voice called from the back. "How old are you anyway?"

Uncle David frowned and clenched his fists.

Before his uncle could intervene, Josh said, "I believe a person should not simply be an evolutionist or a creationist, but instead should be a science scholar. Based on clear evidence, which I'll talk about in a moment, I am convinced that God created the earth. Now, the sets of footprints—"

Someone said, "That's what's wrong with the Scopes Trial. Religious people are afraid science will disprove creation. They're afraid they'll find out God doesn't exist."

"Maybe they are afraid." Josh shoved his hands in his pockets. "Or maybe they're concerned that some people will think evolution is a fact and as a result, decide there is no God."

Several students nodded.

"But I think they're more afraid of something else—and that's science."

Some cocked their heads or raised their eyebrows.

Josh stepped away from the podium. "Science is a mystery to the average person. But it doesn't have to be. In fact, I've got a theory about that."

The students looked interested, so he plunged ahead. "What's the best way to spot a counterfeit?"

"Bite it to see if the coin is fake metal."

Laughter.

Another student said, "Know what the real thing is, and compare."

"Yes!" Josh pointed at the student. "Yes! It's to show the real thing right next to the counterfeit. Side by side. I think teaching evolution next to creation displays which is truth, and which is fake. The evidence points to a Creator. To God."

"Here, here!" a few called out.

"Do you believe in a flood that covered the earth?" another student asked.

Josh folded his arms. "I'm not here to talk about that, but quickly, yes, I do. Fossils and trees are found in sedimentary rock, exactly what I'd expect to find with a global flood. What about sand and mud deposits? Today, we only see thin layers added on the edge of continents, so how were those layers added to the *center* of a continent? Only a global flood could disturb something so massive."

Josh picked up the packet of pictures from the desk. "I have photos here that show humans and dinosaur footprints together in the same strata. Some of the actual evidence in this location has been destroyed, but the photos still exist."

He held them higher and continued, his voice growing stronger and more confident by the minute. "Dr. Hubbard has some pictures of the expedition as well. But these twelve are mine. And I have the negatives to prove that the photos have not been altered. They also include pictures of the men who destroyed the evidence."

The room burst with voices calling out.

Professor Thomas just stared.

Josh returned the photos to the desk. "Let's talk today about what this new, but old, evidence means."

He drew on the chalkboard as he talked. "The human prints were thirteen to fifteen inches long."

He drew the dinosaur track. "The Coelophysis tracks were closer to six inches with clearly defined impressions of three toes. The human prints had no toe definition at all. The human prints were consistent with walking strides, while the dinosaur tracks were spaced far enough apart to indicate running. I believe hunting."

He drew a rough picture of the ibex. "This ibex is drawn on the walls of the canyon. Some archeologists in the group said they were local goats which were drawn with accented horns. But why would you say, 'this can't be a picture of an African animal, because that animal wasn't in America,' but then come up with wild ideas about what you think it could be?" He shook his head. "The dinosaur pictograph is my favorite. It cannot be anything but a dinosaur."

Chatter filled the room.

"Why," he asked when it quieted, "do we throw away evidence because it doesn't fit our preconceived ideas. Stay open to new evidence. Thanks for letting me talk. I'll be here for questions."

Applause filled the room, and as it quieted, he raised his voice so all could hear.

He held up the file. "Uncle David, what would you like

me to do with these pictures?"

His uncle motioned toward the desk. "Just leave them on the desk for tonight so people can get a look at them. I'll have Emma file them in the morning."

"Even the negatives?"

"Just leave them in the envelope with the photos."

Josh set them on the desk. "Thanks for letting me speak. And please do be careful with these. They are our only copies."

"Josh! Thanks for coming!" The student that approached was a tall, dark-haired man with sweater and tie. "Your talk was refreshing."

"No, it wasn't," another student said, shoving past the others that were coming close to get a look. "You didn't explore all the possibilities. Those human prints could be from a dinosaur—one we just haven't found the remains to yet."

"Fossil remains don't match those prints," Josh said. "But yet, there are no ibex fossils or prints, either. Or goats with heads and horns shaped like in the paintings." Josh shrugged. "Our information is incomplete. And that's why this is so much fun. Seeing the evidence and searching for explanations is what makes science so valuable."

Abby watched the students mob Josh.

While he was busy talking, Professor Thomas was the first to pass by and look over the photos. His smirk told her all she needed to know. He'd seen that he wasn't clearly shown in the pictures. He handed them to the nearby students.

Abby heard Dr. Michaels's voice nearby. "Well? This was

a disaster."

"Why would you say that?" Uncle David crossed his arms.

Dr. Michaels looked at Josh. "Confusing students' minds."

Uncle David was about to say something when Professor Thomas weaved his way through the students. "Dr. Hunter, any time creationists look smart, science has failed. They want to destroy science and scientists. It's a war. Between us—and them." He lowered his voice, but Abby could still hear. "This boy may seem smart. But he's dangerous. Both of the children." He glanced down at her.

Uncle David sucked in his breath. "Now, see here..."

Dr. Michaels smiled and patted Uncle David's back. "Professor Thomas is partially right. You're an able teacher. I'm sure that tomorrow you'll fix the damage this boy has done." He gave Miss Emma a kiss on the cheek. "I've got papers to grade, dear, then I'm calling it a night. We'll see you two tomorrow."

"Goodnight," Miss Emma and Uncle David said at the same time, although they both sounded strained. Abby understood why they'd be furious with Professor Thomas, but they didn't seem very happy with Miss Emma's father, either.

Professor Thomas's blond hair slipped into his eyes and he brushed it off his forehead as he stepped between Abby and Uncle David. "Our students' minds aren't able to handle such...confusing ideas. Creationists can't be scientists. They're too caught up in myths based on religious texts."

"Josh just proved that isn't true." Uncle David stared at the other professor.

"I saw those pictures. There's no proof."

Uncle David stepped close and lowered his voice. "Look, you and I've known each other for a long time. Been through a lot together. College. The war. You know me, stop pretending you don't. You know when I'm telling you the truth. I saw the real thing, Professor Thomas. I saw the pictographs of ibex with my own eyes." Uncle David's voice went soft. "Josh and Abby are scientists too, and their opinion on evidence matters."

Professor Thomas's face turned the color of a "They're children. And you're a fool." Professor Thomas shouldered him aside and stormed out.

Miss Emma gasped. "Well, I never."

Uncle David shared a knowing look with Abby. "He's far more emotional about this than an innocent person would be."

Abby nodded. Professor Thomas was anything but innocent.

When the last person walked out the door, Abby began to bounce about the classroom like a crazy kangaroo. "Josh, you were amazing! Did you see how interested everyone was? Even the professors." Her braid slipped from around her head and flapped about her shoulder as she jumped up and down. "What do you think, Uncle David?"

He put a hand on Josh's shoulder. "I'm proud of him, very proud. You'd make a great teacher."

Abby nodded. "And how!"

Uncle David looked at his clock on the wall. "Time for you three to go home. Miss Emma will walk with you. The police should be here any moment. Remember to put a wood stick in each of the windows to secure them. Saw off one of the broom handles if you must."

Walking the two blocks home, Miss Emma gave orders. "Josh, you find sticks that will work on the windows. You heard David. He has several old brooms in the shed out back.

Saw them to size if you need to. Abby, you install them. Make sure the sticks are wedged in tight so that no one can lift the windows. I'm going to stop at the market for bread before they close. Someone burned the last of it in the toaster."

"I'm sorry!" Abby said. "It's just hard to work the lever, and I never notice if I made it stick or not, then I get distracted."

"Sure wish we could have stayed to help Uncle David." Josh kicked a rock off the sidewalk.

"It's not a place for children." Miss Emma opened the gate, and they approached the front door. She unlocked the knob, then let them in. After a quick look around, she said, "I'll be right back. Get to work on those sticks."

Josh walked into the kitchen, scratched a few words on a piece of paper, then set it on the kitchen table. Abby peered over the note.

Miss Emma, went to help Uncle David. We'll stay out of trouble.

Josh

CHAPTER NINETEEN
May, 1925 - Five Minutes Later
Biology Building, Colbey College

Oh, this is wrong, Abby thought. But still, she followed Josh.

They crept from bush to tree across the campus, the evening sun gone and the last vestiges of light illuminating Josh's back.

"I know a window that's always left open," Abby admitted. "It's on the opposite side of Uncle David's classroom, and I see it a lot. That way we don't have to go through the front door."

Josh stepped to the side. "Lead the way."

"Are we going to get in trouble, Josh?"

"Which is worse? A scolding? Or Uncle David sitting in the Biology Building with only the police to help. Besides," he'd added, "Uncle David telling us to stay home was a suggestion, for our safety. But his safety is what *we* are worried about."

"Maybe." She still felt unsettled.

"And there's this. If something happened to him, we'd never forgive ourselves. We weren't there to protect Mom and Dad. We need to be there for him."

She made a fist and smacked it into her open hand. "Let's go."

They entered the park-like area around the biology building, crept under the wide canopy of trees that blocked the starlight, pushed through a thick wall of bushes, and cautiously approached the biology building. The shadow of a window stood open, just like she'd noticed when exploring a while back.

"All right, Abby," Josh said in too loud a voice. "Time to do your stuff. Get us inside."

"*Shh!* Josh! Keep your voice down." She grabbed a branch and swung up into the tree. She pulled on the window, the top part opening out a few more inches. The hinges at the bottom squeaked.

She slipped a foot into the open window, searched down, down, down with the toe of her shoe, until she hit a hard surface. And put her weight down.

In seconds, she stood on a table in the dark room. "All right, come on," she whispered through the window.

She helped direct Josh's foot to the table, and he lowered

himself into the room. "Leave the window open," Abby said, sliding off the table. "I think this is where the intruder will come in. They would have noticed that window is always open."

The classroom was small, clean, with only a few pictures Abby couldn't quite make out in the darkness. A podium stood at the front, and twenty desks sat in perfect rows. The room had a musty smell, as if it wasn't used much. Perhaps that was why they kept the window open.

They hunkered under the desks. The door to the hallway was slightly open, and from Abby's vantage point, she could see dim shadows in the hall lit by outside streetlamps through the large front windows.

The shadow of the massive grizzly bear crossed the door. Her mouth went dry.

Not a sound drifted through the halls and into the classroom. The only smell was dust and cleaning agents. She wrapped her arms around her body and rocked forward and back, almost hitting her head on the desk above.

She had to go to the bathroom. Why, when she had to wait for something to happen, did the urge always hit her?

Right now, Josh was probably thinking of a scientific math formula that illustrated how tension plus darkness equaled the need to go to the bathroom.

Her heart thumped against her chest as she listened for an intruder. It was strange, thinking of Uncle David and the police hiding in his classroom. If they got in trouble, all she needed to do was yell, and he'd come running.

But what if she'd guessed wrong? If the person stealing the pictures was working with Professor Thomas, then he'd have access to a key for the front door. But she'd felt so sure that the intruder would take precautions and sneak in another way, in case someone was watching the front door.

Movement flickered outside the window and a face appeared. The light from the streetlamps was brighter outside the window. She was about to scream for Uncle David when Josh gripped her arm. As the man crept through the window into the room, she wondered if she shouldn't have given Herbert Hoover and his FBI men a phone call.

In the dim light from outside, she saw only a vague shadow of a man. His shoes clicked against the floor. The shadow crossed the room.

Abby held her breath for a few moments. Then she released a stream of air.

A cigar smell drifted across the room, as if he'd just been smoking. She heard the man smacking his chewing gum.

The intruder paused. After a moment, he continued out of the classroom, slipping through the half-open doorway as silently as a ghost—not that she'd ever seen a ghost.

Josh tugged on her sleeve, and she slid from under the desk. She followed him into the hallway. From here, she could see much better from the two lamps right outside the double doors down the hall.

She and Josh weaved around the rhinoceros and paused as the man stood near the grizzly with its splayed paws. Glints of light reflected off the bear's claws, teeth, and eyes.

Josh ducked behind the penguin display as the man opened Uncle David's classroom door and stepped inside. Abby bumped into Josh, and was able to see into the classroom.

The man walked straight for the desk.

There was just enough light to see he wasn't wearing

mobster clothes.

The man reached into his coat pocket and pulled something out. A soft click was followed by a beam of light that settled on the skeleton. The burglar gasped, then chuckled and turned his light toward the desk.

"Jenkins." Uncle David's voice boomed through the classroom and into the corridor.

Abby jumped.

Uncle David called again. "Get away from that desk."

Now Abby remembered the guy. He was the student who'd argued with Josh during the first Darwin Club meeting, the one who'd called Josh "fatso."

Jenkins dropped the flashlight, his silhouette lit by the spinning light on the desk. "Dr. Hunter."

Uncle David stepped into view. "Why are you here?" Two other men appeared beside him, shining flashlights on the student's face.

Jenkins grasped the file of pictures in his hands. "I...I..." He dropped the pictures and jumped forward, lowered his shoulder, and slammed into Uncle David's midsection. Uncle David toppled into the two deputies. They fell into a pile of arms and legs. Flashlight beams bounced throughout the room.

Jenkins jumped to his feet and sprinted for the doorway, straight at Abby. She screamed, "Stop him!"

Josh jumped in front of the would-be thief and hunkered low, like football players readying for a tackle.

Jenkins collided with him, grunting as he rolled head over heels. The college student jumped to his feet, but his leg gave way. He stumbled but regained his balance and half-limped, half-ran toward the exit.

Uncle David and the policemen were still untangling next to the desk.

Abby charged after him but stopped short when the hall lights flickered on. Momentarily blinded, she blinked and saw Emma standing near the front door, her hand on the light switch.

Jenkins bolted the opposite direction, right at Josh again.

Josh threw himself in front of the guy's legs, and Jenkins slammed onto the marble floor.

Just as Uncle David and the deputy burst from the classroom, Jenkins scrambled to his feet and sprinted down the hall. Straight for the window and his final plan for escape. Straight for Abby, who stood waiting for him between the rhinoceros and the penguins.

Jenkins held out his hand as if to shove her out of his way. She grabbed his outstretched arm, crouched, and rolled backward, her feet on his chest. Using his momentum, she heaved him up and over her body. He flew through the air and slammed on his back onto the hard marble floor, landing with a heavy thud.

Uncle David and the police managed to get Jenkins pinned, stomach down, to the ground. He didn't try to escape.

Abby moved close. She glared at him, then let him have it. "I know Judo. You can't run from me. You survived this time. Next time, you may not be so lucky. Did you kill my Mom? Huh? No one thinks I know judo, but I do. Did you kill my Dad? You'd better answer. I know Judo." Her breath came in huge gasps.

Miss Emma grasped Abby and looked into her eyes. "Are you all right? Hey, Abby. It's okay. It's okay."

"I know judo!"

"Abby, look at me." Miss Emma gripped harder.

Abby noticed Josh still crumpled on the ground, holding his head. "Josh! Are you okay?" She broke from Miss Emma and dropped by her brother's side.

Uncle David stepped close and bent over him. "Let me see."

Josh slowly took his hand away from the side of his head.

Uncle David grunted. "You're going to have a nice goose egg there. How bad does it hurt?"

Josh tried to grin, but it turned into a grimace. "Getting injured isn't as fun as it looks."

Miss Emma put her arm around Josh. "I'll take care of him. David, you take care of *him*." She nodded to where the deputies held Jenkins.

Uncle David patted Josh on the back and then turned to the intruder. "Jenkins, you've got some explaining to do. Who sent you?"

His face pressed against the stone, Jenkins mumbled, "No one."

"This isn't something you would think up yourself. I'll see to it you're expelled from Colbey College. I'll also file charges. You're looking at possible jail time, mister. Those pictures mean nothing to you. You weren't at the talk tonight. So, how did you know to steal the pictures?"

"A fellow asked me to get them! Never seen him before tonight."

Uncle David hunkered down, closer to Jenkins' face. "Some nameless guy. That's all you can tell us?"

The deputy shoved Jenkin's arms higher.

"Stop," he cried. "I'll talk. It's true. I never saw him before. He came up to me as I was leaving my dorm room tonight, said I could earn a hundred clams and a swig of bootleg if I nabbed your pictures. I took 'em for the jack."

One of the deputies shook his head. "What does that mean?"

Abby piped up. "One hundred dollars and a drink of alcohol to steal the photos."

The deputy rolled Jenkins over and patted him down. He pulled fifty dollars from the college student's shirt pocket. He patted down his pants. "He's clean. No weapons."

Uncle David pointed to the cash. "How did you come by this much money?"

"Fifty before, and another fifty after I give him the photos."

Uncle David let out a deep breath. He glanced at both police officers. Abby saw one nod, and Uncle David leaned back. "All right, I'm done with him."

That was it? This guy was after them! Abby stamped her foot next to Jenkins's head. "Give me five minutes with him. I'll get the information we need."

The deputy shook his head and lifted Jenkins to his feet. "We'll question him at the department."

Abby couldn't let it go that easily. "Look, mister, I don't think you meant to do much harm, but these guys..." She swallowed. "These men you work for, they killed my mom and dad. Anything you can tell us will help us catch them."

The boy's shoulders sagged. "I'm sorry, kid. Tough break. I might be able to give a description, but like I said, I don't know nothing. Honest."

The police took Jenkins down the hall and out the door. Abby sat on the edge of the penguin display.

Uncle David groaned. "I'd hoped we'd learn more." He shook his head. "Well, I suppose I'd better get the pictures."

He trudged slowly toward his classroom, past Miss Emma and Josh, who leaned against the wall. Abby jumped up and followed. In the light, the animals were far less scary. The bear actually looked friendly and welcoming now, as if he wanted a hug. Maybe, when no one else was around, she would—

"You! Stop!" Uncle David charged into his classroom, and Abby ran after him. A man stood at Uncle David's desk with the packet of pictures in his hand.

The light from the hall showed off his face. "It's him," Abby shouted, "the intruder!"

The man jumped the first row of desks, then the second in a giant leap.

Uncle David tore after him.

The mobster climbed a low shelf under the bank of windows. One window was open, and the intruder squeezed his body through, first his head and chest, then his round belly.

Uncle David grasped the mobster's leg with one hand, boot with the other. Abby ran over to help, but in this case, her judo wouldn't help. Half the man's body hung a few feet over the ground under the window, the other suspended by Uncle David's grip. They had him.

Abby heard Josh and Miss Emma come into the room behind her.

Uncle David's face was red. Not red from strain, or from lack of sleep.

No, he was mad.

Uncle David leaned over and hissed, "Who killed my brother?"

Abby took a step back.

The man struggled.

Uncle David twisted his leg. "Who killed my brother?"

The thief yelled. "I don't know what you're talking about."

"Why did you take the pictures?"

When he didn't reply, Uncle David twisted harder. The man cried out but still didn't answer.

Abby turned away.

"Abby…"

She glanced at her uncle. He had calmed.

He smiled and winked. "Abby, quick, hand me the tarantula terrarium."

Abby followed his gaze. A mounted tarantula was set in a display.

"You won't get anything out of me." Although the words were tough, the man struggled under Uncle David's grip.

"The spider will start under your pant leg..." he paused. "Then crawl up your calf, behind your knee and up your thigh."

The man kicked. "I don't know who killed your brother!"

Abby set the spider within Uncle David's reach.

Uncle David shook his head, then readjusted his grip. "Tell me, who killed my brother?" He touched the man's exposed skin between his pants and his boot and tapped his fingers on his leg with a feather-light touch.

The mobster moaned.

"Who killed them?"

When he didn't respond, Abby gasped and said, "Uncle David, that's a *huge* spider!" She held a hand over her mouth to stifle a laugh.

Her uncle's fingers inched up the man's calf.

"Stop!" he shouted. "I don't know who killed them. Maybe Johnny. Or Slim. All I know is I didn't get the order."

Abby pressed her fingers tighter against her mouth. It *was* these men who'd killed Mom and Dad.

"Who do you work for?" Uncle David demanded. "Who's paying you?" He ran his fingers like a spider over the man's leg.

Josh came up beside him. "Whoa, look at the size of that spider!"

"No!" the intruder screamed. He jerked his leg again and his foot slipped from the boot. Pictures in hand, he scrambled through the bushes and disappeared.

"Let him go." Miss Emma gripped Uncle David's arm. "He's got the pictures and the negative. Once they see them, they won't bother us anymore. That was the plan. Remember?"

Abby threw herself into her uncle's arms. "I heard what he said. About the order to kill Mom and Dad. That's horrible."

He held her close.

Abby exchanged a look with Josh. She knew what he was thinking. The person who hired them were behind Mom and Dad's murder.

Professor Thomas was a killer, or she would eat her pith helmet. Now…how to prove it?

Some things would have to wait.

CHAPTER TWENTY

July, 1925 - Two Months Later
Dayton, Tennessee

Since the mobsters had left them alone for the rest of the school year, Josh had time to read up on the Scopes Monkey Trial, or, as it was officially called, *The State of Tennessee vs John Thomas Scopes*.

The town council in Dayton, Tennessee, had decided to test a new law that said high school teachers could not teach evolution. Testing the law, the council hoped, would make the town famous, and tourists would come see the trial.

They asked a substitute teacher and football coach named

John Scopes to teach evolution so he could be arrested. They promised to provide the best lawyers at no cost to him and with all the backing the American Civil Liberties Union, or ACLU, could provide.

Their plan worked. The entire country talked of Dayton, Tennessee, and their trial.

Josh and Abby followed Uncle David and Miss Emma through Dayton.

Sweat trickled down Josh's back as they wove through the crowds. The hot evening seemed to do little to dampen the festivities. The smell of cooking meat made his stomach rumble.

Abby reached out and took Josh's hand. He glanced down to see she was a little overwhelmed. He gripped tight, then let go. He noticed Miss Emma had taken Uncle David's hand for support.

His uncle was going to provide evidence before the court, that evolution was fact. Abby had asked him earlier if he thought Uncle David would testify.

He explained it to her this way—scientific method entailed coming up with a hypothesis—a guess. Then that hypothesis had to be tested by several scientists. If the results appeared positive, the hypothesis became a theory. Eventually, if no doubts arose, no questions, the hypothesis became a law. Not a law in the legal sense, but one like the law of gravity or Kepler's Laws of Planetary Motion.

Would Uncle David testify that evolution was a hypothesis or a theory or a law?

They followed their uncle as he wormed his way between men with straw hats and women in floral-patterned dresses. They passed by a banner that said *Read Your Bible*. Other signs called out for the anti-evolution league to unite. About fifty people stood in a circle with signs that Josh was about to read when he noticed Abby had fallen behind.

Uncle David stopped at the corner and turned to glance back at them. He seemed in his own world, but Josh couldn't be upset with him. Entering your opinion in a court of law was consuming.

Miss Emma turned, smiled, and winked.

They listened to a man preach on the street corner for a few moments. Josh watched his uncle's reactions as the man called anyone who could hear to repent. God wasn't happy with them because they believed in evolution. Uncle David sighed.

Josh wasn't entirely sure how he felt about the man's message. Evolution was wrong, he had no doubt. But the way he was talking didn't seem to reach Uncle David at all.

They moved on.

Bibles were sold at stands. At a smaller table, a bookseller sold Darwin's book on the evolution of the species. Uncle David paused, reached out, picked up a different book, and showed it to Josh and Abby. *His* book…Uncle David's. Josh smiled.

He was proud of his uncle, but he wished he hadn't written a book about evolution. He'd read the book, twice. At least Uncle David hadn't spent all his time trying to disprove creation. He'd simply interpreted evidence for the sake of evolution.

At the end of the street, under a tree, Uncle David paused and looked into Miss Emma's eyes. Abby and Josh stopped beside him. "You know," their uncle said, shaking his head. "Evolution doesn't have all the answers. But if these churchgoers are hoping to win over scientists, this isn't the way to do it."

Abby frowned. "Then how do we do it?"

He put a hand on her shoulder. "Ask this guy." He rubbed Josh's hair. "Josh has the right idea. He speaks the scientist's language." He sighed. "Let's go find the defense headquarters and get this over with."

But when he started walking again, it seemed as if he walked under water.

Something was wrong with him. Very wrong.

Abby must have felt the same. "Uncle David? Is everything okay?"

He winced. "No, not really."

"You want to sit down?" Miss Emma asked. "There's a bench right there."

He fell onto the bench and put his head in his hands. Abby sat beside him, Miss Emma on the other side, and Josh stood nearby.

People seemed to be drifting toward downtown restaurants and street venders, and their side of town grew quiet.

A screen door slammed at a house, and a car raced past.

"Since the two of you came into my life, you've done nothing but give me trouble." He winked, then laughed. "I expected to marry Emma, write more books, and tour the world talking about biology and evolution. Then you two came along, and you question the very foundation of my beliefs. You ask me questions about evolution and the age of the earth…questions I cannot answer. And you're so good at those questions that someone out there is determined to silence you two. They're willing to hire hit men to see that your work is destroyed."

Josh grimaced. In one way, the way his uncle put it made him feel important. In another, he felt vulnerable.

"There isn't a moment that goes by that I don't miss your dad. But the time I spend with you…" Uncle David's voice caught. "The time I've spent with you two has been spectacular. You've taught me so much, not only about science and fieldwork, but about how to be a better person. How to question and test my beliefs, no matter where it might take me."

He lowered his head again. "I'm about to testify that evolution is the answer to the origin of the species…and I have to take an oath." He blew out a long breath. "An oath to tell the truth. I'm not sure I can say evolution is the truth." He laughed. "There, I said it. You've thrown doubt on all my hallowed theories."

Abby hugged him. "Mom and Dad always said to go with your conscience when you're in doubt."

"That's wise."

She jumped up from the bench. "My conscience wants ice cream."

Uncle David and Miss Emma laughed. "Maybe in a bit. Let's find that mansion first."

They wandered to the edge of town until they found the right house. Report-ers surrounded the veranda, and people chatted quietly on the wide front porch. No wonder the defense made this their headquarters, Josh thought. The house was huge. And there were a lot of people talking in groups.

Several reporters spotted Uncle David and rushed over. "Dr. Hunter, can I have a quote?" asked one. Another asked to take his picture.

"Science moves forward, despite politics," Uncle David mumbled. The reporters scribbled with brown pencils on their notepads. A camera flashed.

"What do you think of the judge not allowing scientific testimony into the trial?"

Uncle David paused with one foot on the porch stair. "What?"

"Haven't you heard?" The reporter seemed eager to dish the news. "The judge just announced it a few moments ago. The trial is about whether Mr. Scopes broke the law teaching evolution. Not evolution. There's no need for scientific testimony."

Uncle David looked at Josh and Abby, relief obvious in his eyes.

"That's exactly right." An older man with a bulldog face stepped close. "The defense is a platform for evolutionary thinking. And the country is watching." He held out his hand. "Clarence Darrow, for the defense. We've no leg to stand on. The trial's over when it resumes Monday. The jury will no doubt hand Mr. Scopes a guilty verdict."

Uncle David shook the man's hand and gave his name. "My fiancé is Emma Michaels. So, I'm not needed?"

"Daughter of Dr. Michaels? Honored you are here, too. Dr. Hunter, you *are* needed. We're taking testimony right now and entering evidence into the records, so that when we appeal, the records will include all the scientific facts. Come on in. You and Miss Michaels."

Josh and Abby followed right behind him.

"Looks like you brought your children." Mr. Darrow smiled.

Uncle David looked back. Josh expected him to explain how their parents died.

Instead, he said, "You don't mind, do you?"

"Mind? Of course not. That's what this fight is about! Children's minds. Come in, come in."

Josh glanced at his sister. Abby smiled.

Inside, the house was hot, even though the windows were open. The sound of their shoes tapping against the hardwood floor seemed to silence all other noise. Men of all sorts, some fat, some skinny, some with hair, others bald, and some with nice smiles, talked in clusters throughout the house. Were Miss Emma and Abby the only girls? As Uncle David passed by, the people in rooms grew quiet. Some men whispered.

Mr. Darrow led them into a small room. "Cooler in here." He pointed through the open window. "Thanks to that big shade tree. Nice, right?"

Uncle David didn't respond.

A desk with typewriter sat in the center of the room, and a small man sat behind it, reading. He set his book down.

"Ah, young scholars, here to testify?"

Josh smiled but turned when he heard a sound behind him and saw people cramming in the hallway. He glanced at Uncle David, who was eyeing the onlookers, a wary expression on his face. Josh peeked out the door. Fifty? One hundred people? One bazillion?

Mr. Darrow patted a chair in front of the desk. "Charles, this is Dr. Hunter."

The man behind the desk stood. "No need for introductions." He pumped Uncle David's hand vigorously.

"And this is Dr. Michaels's daughter."

"Miss Michaels, an honor." He grasped her hand.

The clerk took his chair and set his hands on his typewriter. He started clicking at the keys. "Dr. David Hunter. The best biologist this nation has." He looked up and smiled.

Mr. Darrow motioned to the seat by the desk. "Sit here, Professor. I'll get a couple more chairs for Miss Michaels and…dear me, what are your names?"

"I'm ape." Josh pointed to his sister. "And this is chimpanzee." The words had just slipped out.

Mr. Darrow scratched his head for a second, then burst

out laughing, as did the dozens of men filling the hallway. Despite their laughter, Josh felt a foul mood coming on like a storm. They had crossed into enemy territory. What was Uncle David going to do?

His uncle glanced again at the crowds behind him and then turned to Mr. Darrow. "Why are they here?"

Mr. Darrow slapped Uncle David on the back. "They've all read your book, Dr. Hunter. They're here to listen to you! I'll go get a couple more chairs." He left the room.

"Abby," Uncle David whispered. "I need a drink. Could you find me some water?"

She nodded and followed Mr. Darrow from the room, the summer skirt Miss Emma had talked her into wearing swishing as she went.

"All right," the thin man at the desk said, pulling his type-writer closer. "While we wait, let's get started for real. First, your name."

"Dr. David Hunter."

"Occupation."

"I teach biology at Colbey College in Colbey, Tennessee. I'm also an author of several scientific papers and a book."

"Hobbies."

He frowned. "What do my hobbies have to do with any-thing?"

The man motioned with his head. "They're listening," he whispered. "Let's make this interesting. Hobbies."

Uncle David cleared his throat. "Well, I like to read. And I have a fiancée."

Miss Emma laughed. "Thank you, Darling. Are you go-ing to marry science?"

Laughter filled the hall.

Abby followed Mr. Darrow back into the room and handed a glass of water to her uncle. Mr. Darrow arranged the chairs against the wall and motioned them to sit, which they did. Uncle David took a long drink and set the glass on the desk.

Mr. Darrow remained standing. "Dr. Hunter, I will have the clerk ask you a few questions. I've provided Mr. Charles with a list, and since I'm going to save my voice for court tomorrow, he'll do the talking."

Josh wasn't so sure Mr. Darrow could keep quiet for five seconds.

He continued. "If there is anything else you'd like to add, or if a certain question has not been asked that you'd like to inject, just say so. We can accommodate. To set the stage, the Butler Act, which prohibits the teaching of evolution in high schools—does it make sense to you?"

Uncle David sat on the edge of his seat. "In my opinion, that law does not make sense. Why limit knowledge and ideas? Children, if taught correctly, can think for themselves."

Josh glanced out the door. The hallway was packed with unusually quiet men, who appeared to be barely breathing, hanging on every word.

"Is evolution fact or myth?"

Josh studied his uncle.

The tension in the room seemed to raise the temperature another ten degrees.

Uncle David looked at the hardwood floor and clenched his jaw. A vein bulge in his neck.

After a moment, he looked up. He leaned his elbows on his knees and gestured with his hands as he spoke. "The theory of evolution is simply that, a theory. But what does that mean? Theories, as all scientists know, aren't simply conjectures. They're tried and retried experiments and observations that point to a specific conclusion. In this case, the theoretical conclusion is that man descended from another species. We look at the apparent evidence like a misshaped skull and some believe it points toward this theory."

Josh stared at his uncle. What was wrong? He sounded like he was writing a book, not giving evidence? Miss Emma and Abby stared at him as well. His voice was monotone. Lifeless. He wouldn't seem to make eye contact with anyone. Usually, he was so dynamic.

He looked at Abby and then at Josh and muttered, "Dr. Michaels will fire me for this." He sat back, squared his shoulders, and took a deep breath. Then he said in a loud voice. "I cannot testify under oath that evolution is true. I'm sorry, but I no longer have faith in my belief of evolution. I will not continue."

Murmurs filled the hallway.

Mr. Darrow thrust his thumbs into his suspenders. "My dear man, are you saying...?" His voice changed from friendly to concerned. His chin lowered. "That everything you wrote in your marvelous book is untrue? Because you certainly sounded convinced at the time. A very convincing book, I might add, one read and trusted by tens of thousands of readers."

"What I wrote in the book is how I interpreted the evidence—the clues—available at that time. But since then..." He smiled at Josh, then Abby. "But since that time, I've looked at other archeological findings and I see many proofs for creation."

Voices grew louder.

Uncle David stood and slipped into professor mode. "I saw dinosaurs carved on a canyon wall in Arizona. Not drawings of bones, but flesh and blood the artist undoubtedly saw first, then drew. The beasts were standing, which means they were alive at the time they were recorded in these drawings. Human beings observed and depicted living, breathing dinosaurs. I also saw drawings of ibex located in the same strata, within feet of a dinosaur. And a drawing of an elephant."

The attorney, with hands on his hips, walked over to

stand directly in front of Uncle David. "Are you saying you no longer believe the theory of evolution is true? You believe *myths* now?"

Josh gripped his knees, ready for the two men to throw punches. With all the watching men eager for controversy, this could turn into all-out bedlam. He'd be ready to defend his uncle the best he could.

Uncle David didn't back away. "Some of the greatest scientists in history accepted the biblical account of creation. Kepler, Bacon, Boyle, Pasteur, Newton, to name a few. Are we to dismiss their proven scientific ideas and theories, which are the basis for much of life and science, because of their beliefs in a Creator?"

"This is preposterous. Ancient history." Darrow, red-faced and jowls flapping, stretched his arms wide. "We're not talking about fairy tales, David. We're talking about hard facts. Truths based on contemporary research and findings." Spit flew from Mr. Darrow's lips.

"That's enough." Uncle David raised his palm. "Cry *fairy tale* all you like, but the truth is, no evidence exists to prove that one species turned into another species. *That*, Mr. Darrow, is the fairy tale." He held out his hand to his niece and fiancée. "Come, Abby, Emma. We must be going." He glanced down at Josh, and they exchanged smiles.

Mr. Darrow grasped Uncle David's shoulder and spun him around. "You're telling me that you, a star witness against creationism, are walking out?" he yelled. "That you will no longer be an evolutionist?"

Uncle David lowered his voice. "I will not rush my conclusions to fit your needs."

"You leave me no choice. Tomorrow, I will call as a witness William Jennings Bryan himself! He's all we have left."

Everyone in the hallway erupted in yelling and questions. Josh, Abby, Uncle David, and Miss Emma hurried out of the building, reporters close behind.

Outside, the air was cooler.

The reporters finally stopped following. As they started for the boarding house where Josh and Uncle David were staying across the street from Miss Emma and Abby's hotel across the street, Uncle David pulled him and Abby close. "You two have opened up a whole new world for me. Thank you for coming into my life. You've made me a stronger-thinking man."

Josh noticed Miss Emma standing to the side, tears welling in her eyes. But he was pretty sure they were happy tears.

"What's next?" Abby pulled away. "Are you sending us to an orphanage?"

Josh stared at his sister. She'd mentioned the thought after Mom and Dad died, but he'd taken it for granted that life would continue as it was now. Although he was interested in the answer, why had Abby asked that now?

As if she was reading his mind, she said, "Because that was the most beautiful speech I ever heard, and think I want to do more things like go to Arizona with you and listen to men and women talk the way you just did." She hugged him. "Please say you'll keep us."

Uncle David glanced at Miss Emma, and she nodded.

Uncle David dropped to a knee. In the noisy evening, still hot and humid, he pulled Josh and Abby close. "I want you to live with me, and when Emma and I marry, with us. That is, if you'd like us to act as not just your guardians, but more like parents. Meaning you'll have some rules."

Josh smiled, and Abby burst into tears. "Oh yes!" she said.

"And don't tell anyone, but I'm thinking of writing a new book. I'll need your help."

Abby wiped her tears away. "About evolution?"

He laughed. "Yes, and about creation. It's going to be a different kind of book, one that looks at arguments for both creation and evolution. Which one will come out on top? I have a lot of research to do. Will you help me?"

That sounded like heaven to Josh. "I've always wanted to see the arches in Utah. I've read that they have petroglyphs carved on them."

"Why stay in the States?" Uncle David stood and grabbed their hands. "We can go anywhere in the world."

Abby shouted, "Woohoo" and danced a circle on the sidewalk, still holding his hand. A dog tied to a nearby tree barked.

Josh paused. "What you did back there, Uncle David, refusing to testify. Will you be in trouble at the college?"

He glanced at Miss Emma again and frowned. "Maybe." He put his hand on Josh's shoulder. "Look, I'm going to put this to you straight. Like your father, my life has always been about telling the truth, no matter the cost. That's how we were raised, and how I know you were raised. Sometimes, that can be hard. And sometimes, you lose your job because you did the right thing."

Josh added quickly, "But Dad always said not to be afraid of doing hard things."

Uncle David stood. "That's right. Do the hard things. So, this summer, where would you like to go?"

Abby was quick to respond. "Africa. I want to see a lion face-to-face, maybe even pet one."

"I'd like to see the dinosaur carvings in Honduras. Maybe go back to Brazil." Josh remembered home. "You know, Mom and Dad had a chest of fossils or something I've always wanted to look through. They kept it locked, and I always wondered if there were things they didn't want us to know about inside. When we asked, they said it was nothing."

"But I saw Dad put a rock in there that was a fossil," Abby said. "I just don't remember what the fossil was."

"Well, then, it may be time to go back to your house and

see what's in that chest."

Josh's step was a little higher as they started to walk along. His mind clicked through encyclopedia entries he wanted to personally research. Oh, there were adventures to come. He could feel it in his bones. And he couldn't wait. A fantastic summer, and then, when they returned to Colbey, he would find out who had hired those mobsters that killed Mom and Dad.

Miss Emma took Abby's hand, Abby held Uncle David's, then Josh held on, and the four of them walked down the street together.

History

Josh and Abby lived in thrilling times. 1925 in America was a time of invention and exploration.

What were Josh and Abby's lives like before their trip to Arizona and Havasu Canyon? When younger, they would walk to the theater and watch Charlie Chaplain in silent movies. Josh read the screen and whispered the lines to Abby.

On the radio at home, Josh and Abby listened to news reports about explorers marching to the North and South Pole. Josh loved hearing about Shackleton's explorations.

The song "Tea for Two" hit the top of the charts. Neither Josh nor Abby liked jazz much, but Josh preferred the music played when his parents took him to the chamber orchestra on the other edge of town, where they played Bach or added more brass and played like a march band. Sousa was the best. Abby liked piano music—Chopin especially. She loves it when Uncle David plays piano. Especially the haunting Nocturne.

Their parents bought a radio phonograph that played discs, and sound came from a large bell or trumpet. The disc was of someone playing Chopin and Rachmaninoff piano music. Of course, it wasn't as good as Uncle David playing.

Engines were better, stronger, and cheaper, so many people owned cars. Uncle David's car cost $290. But there were no driver's licenses. Josh learned to drive when his dad was tinkering with engines, and his dad asked for Josh to start the car. It was a short step to drive just a little way, down the driveway. And finally, Josh could drive. By that point, Josh had worked with cars for a year.

Josh remembered when a telephone was installed in their house, and Abby thought she recalled.

Before 1920, people could drink alcohol, but a constitutional amendment in 1920 said that drinking was prohibited. You could still see people drinking, but they did so against the Prohibition laws.

Josh and Abby both remember when women won the right to vote in 1920 They walked with their mother and father to the voting booth at the library, and they all sang the *Star-Spangled Banner*, and their mother cried as she marked her ballot.

Josh and Abby heard people talking about World War I, but Josh didn't remember much about the war. Their father and Uncle David were gone for a year. But when Josh asked his dad what he did, his dad said he didn't go overseas. He worked as a supply officer in the United States. But he warned them not to ask Uncle David what happened in the war. Maybe someday Uncle David will tell them.

The war had made airplanes popular. Just before Josh and Abby left for Arizona, Josh was reading in the newspaper how the United States Air Service had circled the globe with its planes.

Uncle David's school and town, Colbey, Tennessee, as well as Colbey College, are fiction. But the town and school are like dozens across America. College students all over America loved Biology Departments, where animals were stuffed and put on display, much like the hall where Josh and Abby are having adventures.

In 1924, Mr. Doheny, a rich oil tycoon, paid Dr. Samuel Hubbard to research the Havasu area in Arizona to study petroglyphs that resemble dinosaurs. That's where Josh and Abby come in. No, Josh and Abby and their parents aren't real, but in our story, they were asked to come along on this very important expedition. You can learn more by checking out the link below.

http://www.creationism.org/swift/DohenyExpedition/Doheny01Main.htm

The discoveries on the canyon walls were photographed by the expedition members, and today the pictures leave evolutionists baffled. A picture of a dinosaur is clear. Just as inexplicable to evolutionists are the other finds that Josh and Abby talk about in the story.

In the Havasupai area, there are no dinosaur tracks next to human tracks that have been discovered, but there are in other locations. In fact, over 30 human and dinosaur track sites are found all over the earth! Texas and British Columbia are two such places. The link below is a list Josh would have loved to research.

http://www.footprintsinstone.com

On March 21st, 1925, Josh and Abby were in Arizona with their parents, building scaffolding up the Havasu wall, when the Butler Act in Tennessee made it illegal to teach evolution in the state.

John Scopes, a football coach, was substituting for science class. He taught evolution, which at the time, was against the law. His case went to trial in what was an enormous affair,

Scope's side saying the law banning the right to teach evolution was ridiculous. The other side said it was illegal to teach evolution and were baffled by the need for some people to teach there was no God. The two sides didn't quite understand each other.

Uncle David, while fictional, represents one of many experts who were called to attempt to prove that science was the answer—that evolution was true—and the Butler Act was wrong. At first, the two sides brought witnesses to testify, and the case lasted several days. Finally, the judge decided the trial wasn't about evolution. The law was simple. Teaching evolution was illegal. The case was about whether John Scopes taught evolution or not, and scientists weren't needed.

John Scopes was found guilty and fined $100.

Reading the transcripts from the trial and discussing them as a family is a fantastic way to learn more about the debate between evolution and creation!

Josh has an amazing memory, and so can you. Because he didn't have a phone or computer to look up information, he *had* to remember everything. Exercising your memory is vital if you want to remember facts like Josh. A great place to start is to memorize scripture and poetry. Next, read. Lots and lots of reading. You'll find yourself remembering facts and ideas you read. Another good trick is remembering people's names.

No one is sure if the monster Josh read about was real or a myth. There's no doubt, when a person is scared and sees something strange, the memory can play tricks on the brain. Many people believe the Mogollon Monster was an albino grizzly bear that wandered into the canyon. That's what Josh believes.

Many men, like Dr. David Hunter, study science and believe there is no God. Then they see evidence that shakes them to the core. They ask themselves—does a person *have* to believe in science *or* in God? Do science and God fight each other? Not at all. In fact, most scientists, according to a recent survey by Pew Research, believe in a 'Higher Power.' When scientists discover something beyond evolutionary explanations, they keep searching. Some turn to God. Others keep searching, refusing to believe. What will Uncle David do?

Josh and Abby's adventures are just beginning! They hope to see you again soon!

More resources:

To learn more about Creation vs evolution, these organizations have working PHD scientists on staff researching the scientific evidence that supports the Biblical account:

Answers in Genesis
https://answersingenesis.org

The Institute for Creation Research (ICR)
http://www.icr.org

Creation Ministries International
https://creation.com

To find Creation sites, museums, speakers and more, visit:

Creation Network
http://creationnetwork.org

Note from Ken Raney

In the Fall of 2008 I had been considering the story of an evolutionist biology professor who became the legal guardian of two teenage children who'd been raised to be Creationists. I had been through my own search for answers.

I was taught all through school—evolution and billions of years, but as I read the Bible after becoming a Christian in college, it became obvious that the Bible, as written, did not agree. I heard all the options: the Gap Theory which places a gap in time between Genesis chapter 1:1 and verse 2, Theistic Evolution that asks, "Well, couldn't God have used evolution to create the Universe?", to the Day Age Theory which uses the Bible verse "To God a day is like a thousand years, and a thousand years is like a day" to support evolution. But, in the back of my mind, I knew the Bible said that "In the beginning God created… and it was evening and it was morning of the first day." That didn't really seem to need a lot of deciphering or decoding. God did it all in six, 24-hour time periods. The only way I could believe these other "theories" was to either add to the Scriptures or take away from them.

Early on in my Christian walk I took a class called "The Bible and Science," in which we learned that scholars had taken great care to be sure the Scriptures we had today were, indeed the Scriptures that had been handed down to us over the centuries. We learned that over 30,000 manuscripts and fragments had been discovered that could be compared to today's Bibles and that the Dead Sea Scrolls confirmed that the Bible we have is the Bible God wanted us to have. It is truly the Word of God. It has never been proven to be wrong. It has hundreds of prophecies written within it that have been fulfilled (all but the ones about the future, which has not yet happened). Where the Bible touches on science, it has always proved to be correct. Soon, I determined to believe the Scriptures even though I may or may not always understand them, and even if they disagree with popular, secular beliefs.

I have found that in every field of science, the evidence tends to confirm the Biblical account. There are about 100 time "clocks" (such as the amount of salt in the ocean, the buildup of talus at the base of cliffs, the distance of the moon from the earth, the magnetic field of our planet, and many, many more) that indicate that the universe cannot be very old. Probably only thousands of years old. Certainly not billions of years old. We find sedimentary rock all over the planet. There are fossils in those rocks that give every evidence that they were swept up in a flood. A study of languages indicates there are about 70 to 90 original languages, which is what we would determine from the Bible's table of nations listed in Genesis chapter 10. The Bible indicates that the Earth and the entire universe was created out of water, and we find water all over the cosmos.

There are many, many more of these evidences if we care to look. Well, I started looking and realized that young people are not learning the truth—even in church—today. I have always had a heart for young people, having raised a pack of them. So, *Dino Hunters* came about as a way to address this truth deficit.

Peter and I hope the Hunter family will help young (and old) people realize that the Bible is, indeed, the Word of God and that the Bible can be trusted. Every word of it.

Note to parents from Peter Leavell

God makes every child different. Josh and Abby are sensory seekers. Both interact with the world through their senses. Josh, however, feels pain more than what's considered normal, so he shies away from things that might hurt—like jumping and falling. He needs light touch and gentle hugs. He can feel his clothes hanging from his body most of the time. He's more comfortable with books. Abby is the opposite. She feels little pain, so she's working to feel something, anything. She needs rough and tumble hugs, and when bored, she'll just fall out of her chair. Incredibly, she won't cry when her bone is broken.

Science is starting to understand how sensory children think and work. My two children are similar to Josh and Abby, and if you have a sensory seeking child, you'll find it relieving to hear that when your son is beating his head on the wall, it's normal. Of course, stop him and find help, but many times, he's looking to feel something, anything.

My children, after therapy, are somewhat normal. My daughter now can feel pain. And my son can handle pain like a professional.

—

Made in the USA
San Bernardino, CA
23 January 2018